Volume II: Burned by the Inner Sun

BY ANSON MONTGOMERY

CHOOSE YOUR OWN ADVENTURE® THE GOLDEN PATH™
PUBLISHED BY

CHOOSECO®
WAITSFIELD, VERMONT

Cover Painting by Nancy Taplin
Illustrated by Vladimir Semionov
Cover Design by Dot Greene, Greene Dot Design
Book design by Stacey Boyd, Big Eyedea Visual Design

CHOOSECO

For information regarding permission, write to:
P.O. Box 46
Waitsfield, Vermont 05673
www.cyoa.com

ISBN-10: 1-933390-82-4
ISBN-13: 978-1-933390-82-6

Published simultaneously in the United States and Canada

Printed in the United States

0 9 8 7 6 5 4 3 2 1

For Rebecca

North
Big Sur
Carlsbad
Lemurian
Territory
Holeeloh
Light
Home
The Great Cave
Desera Fox
Colony
Troglodytes

CAST OF CHARACTERS

Dresdale Hamilton – One of your two best friends.
Peter Kim – Your other best friend.
Dianna Torman – Your mother. She and your father are missing and presumed to be in the hollow earth.
Donald Torman – Your father.
Dr. Heinrich Schliemann – Head of the Federal Historical Accuracy Board and head of the Carlsbad Caverns expedition. Responsible for your expulsion from school.
Sceptus I – Emeperor of Agartha. He wages a war in the inner world for complete control. Only the Lemurians, The Forgotten People, the Desera and a few others oppose his goal of controlling the whole inner earth.

CARLSBAD BRANCH CHARACTERS

Neila – One of the Illuminated, a group of inner earth beings who glow with an internally created light. You met Neila and two of his companions while exploring the Carlsbad branch.
Relevart - Elder of the Illuminated.
Ediug - An Illuminated who teaches you about the landscape of the inner earth.
Yip & Yap - Peter's nicknames for two Desera Fox people.

BRAM INTERIOUS BRANCH CHARACTERS

Bram Interious – Heir to the Agarthan Empire and soldier. You have an unusual bond with him.
Durno – Your Lemurian guide whom you met in the camp of Sublimas-Chaeko, a Lemurian commander. Durno acts like a combination of a drill sergeant and a dorm head.
Prince Torgan – Leader of the Lemurians in their capital city of Lighthome.
Turina and Keldso – Niece and Nephew of Durno. They journey with you for a while.
Sublimas-Chaeko – Commander of a Lemurian camp and adviser to Prince Togan.

BIG SUR BRANCH CHARACTERS

Lt. Ferris McMann- Member of the FFA and pilot of the "No Name."
Ama – Leader of the Forgotten People.
Tat – A scout of the Forgotten People.
Noaaon – A warrior in the fight against the Agarthans.

NO EMERALD BRANCH CHARACTERS

Alphonse Rimy – A teacher at your former school, he is an old friend of your parents'. He brought you to the inner earth through the North Pole and introduced you to the Lemurians.

TABLE OF CONTENTS

Entrance

You are a student at the Alstone boarding school, with nothing on your mind besides a Trigonometry test the next day, when your life changes utterly in a matter of hours. You and your best friends, Peter Kim and Dresdale Hamilton, are accused of cheating, plagiarism and fraud on a term history paper about a shard of pottery from Carlsbad, New Mexico. The worst thing is that your innocence doesn't seem to matter. The three of you are expelled from school on the trumped up charges brought by Dr. Heinrich Schliemann, head of the Federal Historical Accuracy Board, a shadowy government agency that wields unusual power for its innocuous-sounding name. Taking Peter's car from its hiding spot in town, you and your friends travel alone to your parent's house to regroup.

Upon your arrival, you find that your house is not as it should be. The grisly discovery of your mother's dog, Tito, dead in the garage, and the following disturbing email from your mother set you on the quest to find your parents that will become the Golden Path.

```
FROM: Dianna Torman
dtorman@deadmail.anonymous.guyana.000
SUBJECT: Something has happened to us.

Sweetheart, I don't want to alarm you, but I fear
I must. If you are getting this email it is
because something has happened to us. It is rigged
to be sent from a special "dead drop" anonymous
server if I have not checked back in three days.
Your father and I have been afraid that people
```

were moving against us after we were removed from heading the Carlsbad dig. I can't get too specific because I do not know myself who exactly is targeting us. We will try and contact you as soon as we are able.

Leave school and go see your Uncle Harry in Carlsbad. He works in the branch office of the Federal Historical Accuracy Board and he can help you. His work address is: FHAB District Office, Harold Turner, 224 Mesa Street, Suite B11,Carlsbad, NM.

Don't call him or email him, just go see him as soon as possible!

Use the flyer at home if you can. It has enough fuel to get to Carlsbad, and its transponder codes have been authorized to fly there. Don't try going anywhere else though, as the Gatekeepers will immediately stop you. They keep a tight leash on all flyers.

Rimy can give you a ride home from school; he is a trusted friend. Just tell him I asked him as a "special boon."

I will try and leave a more detailed note in the secret spot. There is much your father and I need to explain to you, but I can't really explain until I see you in person. I can't wait until I see your beautiful face! Be strong, be brave, and know that your father and I love you more than life itself! I am sorry to scare you with this news, but it will all work out in the end!!!!

Love,
Mom

The world that you live in is a dangerous and mysterious one, even for children and young adults. People you know have been taken by the Gatekeepers, a quasi-secret police who monitor movement and information in the United States and Provinces, previously called the United States of America. Some come home. Others don't. Everyone is cautious about what they say and do.

Worldwide changes, caused in part by rising sea levels and extreme weather, have resulted in many wars, government collapses and natural catastrophes. New York City was almost obliterated by a monstrous tsunami and rebuilt as a water city like lost Venice, Italy. Most of Canada and parts of Mexico were absorbed by the United States after it suspended its constitution and instituted emergency rule. That was 13 years ago. You don't remember much about that time, just adults telling you to be quiet and go play in the other room.

Asia and Europe face their own problems and challenges, but quality information is at a premium and you never get the full story. China continues to dominate Eastern Asia under the rule of restored empire, while Russia, flowering in the warming north, causes its own misery by fighting a series of brutal civil wars. Limited nuclear strikes made the drying wells of power in the Middle-East unusable. Now you face all new challenges as you enter the hollow earth in search of your parents. You find many friends, but just as many enemies as you travel through this strange world within.

Depending on your choices in volume one, you faced a variety of obstacles and opportunities. You have the choice of continuing a story you know from volume one, or choosing a new path. If you did not read the first volume, make a choice below based on your instincts and more background information will be revealed when you turn to the story.

Choose wisely; there are four choices below, but there is only one Golden Path!

Choice One

One entrance into the inner earth is through the volcanic tubes and shafts below Carlsbad Caverns in southern New Mexico. The evil Dr. Schleimann, who ordered you expelled from the Alstone School, runs a research center in the caverns. It is here that your parents were supposed to have gone when they disappeared. Neila, an Illuminated, or special glowing being who comes from the inner earth, tries to help you transit into the inner earth through the natural complex of volcanic tubes and shafts.

Neila is ill, contaminated by being on the surface too long. He needs to return to be healed in the inner earth. The Radiant Ones, fire people who destroy at will and are linked with evil, confront you and hunt you and your group both on the earth's surface and in the inner earth.

Are your parents really deep within the earth's crust or is this a huge mistake?

If you want to continue the story of the escape from the burning Radiant Ones in Carlsbad Cavern with Neila, one of the Illuminated, turn to the recap on page 33.

Choice Two

After a bizarre encounter with a man who disappears in a burned town while stopping on your flight to Carlsbad, NM, you don't know what to think. He said he was fighting against the dictatorship in the United States and Provinces as a member of the Freedom Forever Alliance (FFA), a guerrilla group resisting the rule of the US&P Gatekeepers. This 'agent' tells you that your entrance to the inner earth is best accomplished not through the Carlsbad Caverns but through a safer route. He also tells you that your parents were part of the FFA and that your safe zone in Carlsbad has been compromised. Surrounded by the after images of burned residents on the walls, he vanishes into a silver cable and is gone. But before he leaves completely, he tells you to go to a new connection point in Big Sur, in what once was California.

You are functioning on blind trust and gut instinct at this point. Nothing seems normal or real, except that your parents might have been kidnapped. Who can you trust—really?

If you choose this dangerous path, turn to page 52.

Choice Three

Durno, your pale Lemurian guide, leads the way in a headlong race against your pursuers, the forces of Sceptus I, Emperor of Agartha, ruler of more and more of the inner world. The inner earth is a strange, sometimes nightmarish land, but you grow to trust the Lemurians as they resist the might of Sceptus. Durno leads you through the dangers of his world, goading and prodding you like a stern but good-hearted coach. You appreciate his help and guidance, but you resent your dependence on someone else, someone different, in a land that is completely alien to you.

However, you rarely have time to sit and stew about anything, as you are constantly on the run and in danger. While traveling, a mud storm engulfs your part of the inner earth, and you and your friends barely escape death. Your troubles only increase as you are confronted with poison-laden giant bats. You learn that the bats are trained to carry their canisters of poison to contaminate the water supplies of Lemurian cities after you experience a psychic connection with Bram Interious, heir of Sceptus to the Agarthan Empire. For a short time, you ARE Bram Interious. You think his thoughts, inhabit his body, and accept it all as normal. It is like a dream, but everything is true, not mist and shadows.

Your main goal is to find and free your parents, but now you are being brought into the greater conflict between the Agarthans and the few remaining free people of the inner world.

If you want to explore this branch of Burned By The Inner Sun, then turn to page 1, for the recap before the chapter "When in Doubt...".

Choice Four

Traveling through the North Pole maelstrom to get to the inner earth, you faced many challenges getting that far. Gatekeepers, ice jams, and mechanical problems conspired to keep you from your goal, but you managed to make it through somehow. Once inside, you are introduced to the Lemurians, a humanoid but not truly human culture opposing the forces of Sceptus. Sceptus claims that the Lemurians are psychic vampires as his reason for waging his war against them. You, however, see no evidence that they are anything other than a people trying to defend themselves, and besides, Rimy, a teacher from your school who brought you into the inner world, trusts and knows them.

While the guest of the Lemurians in the inner earth, you are offered the unusual honor of undergoing the Truth Enlightenment Ritual by the Lemurian commander, Sublimas-Chaeko. In the ritual, a shard of emerald is to be implanted in your head. Although you like and feel a certain level of trust in your new friends, something makes you hesitant to accept their offer. You decline this honor and have to deal with the consequences of that decision.

If you wish to enter the story in the inner earth, after refusing the Truth Enlightenment Ritual turn to page 29.

Recap of your story so far from *The Golden Path, Vol. 1, Into the Hollow Earth.*

Having made your way into the Hollow Earth with your companions Peter, Dresdale, and Rimy, you meet the Lemurians, opponents of Sceptus I. You are attacked by the forces of Sceptus and forced to flee into the wilderness of the inner world with Durno, your guide, and his helpers. Rimy is left behind to a fate unknown...

From *Volume I, Into the Hollow Earth*, p. 183

Durno is keeping watch tonight. Tired as you are, sleep eludes you.

You nod to him as you slip out of the tent. The sun has dimmed to the point that it is difficult to see color, but you make out objects in this world of half light. Even the reds of the landscape seem to be mere shades of gray.

You navigate the path carefully to the lookout point. Moving down toward the road, you breathe in the coolness of the night air. There are no stars above you. Most of the clouds have drifted to the sides, so all that is giving light is the now dimmed sun. Even dimmed, the sun appears as a bright spark in the sky.

Suddenly, three dark shapes come between you and the sun, casting you briefly into their shadows. The shapes are huge in the sky, and you see great wings beating slowly.

Crouching down to make yourself as unnoticeable as possible, you peer up to see what these flying animals are. The three shapes move out from the ridge and set down on an outcropping of rock only a few hundred feet below you.

Bats. Giant bats. Three dark shapes get off the backs of the huge bats. Metal flashes red in the dim light from the waist of one of the figures. The hood of the one with the glinting metal falls back and you catch sight of his face.

A flash of green light blinds you, and you fall back, dazed. Sitting back up, you see that the three figures have not reacted to the flash of light and are still busy taking supplies off their mounts. The bats' faces are gruesome in the red light. Their folded noses and sharp teeth make them look like moving gargoyles. You look at the figure with the clear face. Once again, you see a wash of green go before your eyes as you see the face of a young man only a few hundred feet away. Your world shifts and you fall into a swirling pool of green light.

The feel of the bat's fur is soft and smells musty, as if you were inside of a cave, instead of out in the open air. Your hands fumble slightly with the clasp of the leather riding harness.

"Move it, Bram," says Morphus in your ear. "We need to have this raid over with before the sun grows bright."

"I know," you say, not really knowing. "I am almost done rigging up the release system."

"You should have done that before, Bram," Morphus hisses. "I thought I trained you better than that. But apparently not. We need to meet with our informer to get the final location of the water processing station. Now you are making me late."

You don't see his hand move, but you feel the sharp blossom of pain from where his dark hand hit the back of your head. Trying to ignore the pain, you focus on setting up the release system. Your momentary clumsiness is gone, and you complete the task quickly.

Looking around, you notice that there is a traveler's shelter above your perch. After meeting the informant, you'll have to go up to clear out any potential witnesses to your presence. Surprise is essential for this mission.

You pull your hood up and follow Morphus and Centurion Afals down the steep path.

You come to not knowing where you are, or who you are. A grinding noise distracts you from your sense of displacement. It's your teeth.

Sitting up, you look down at your hands, and you are relieved that they are the same hands that have always been there, except for a few moments ago, when they were the hands of someone else. Bram, your name had been Bram. 'I have to stop them from poisoning the water supply,' you think.

All three figures have left the outcropping. Left behind are the three bats. They have been hobbled somehow, and they hop about the small space awkwardly. You see the three canisters of poison strapped to their chests. The canisters gleam dully in the light. Something has to be done...

Your story continues...

"When in Doubt..."

A desperate plan forms in your head. You are so close that you feel you could run down to the outcropping, take the canisters off, free the bats from their hobbles, and stop the planned poisoning. You know what sort of destruction is planned, and you can't just wait for it to happen. Besides, Bram said he would come back to look for any witnesses.

What is happening to you? Are you going crazy? How do you know what you know? Why are you thinking like this? Are you just trapped in a dream?

No. What just happened was not a dream. You need to act—now. People's lives are at stake.

Your body pulses with adrenaline. A sense of power and energy fills you with a strange euphoria.

"What is happening?" you mutter to yourself.

Your head fills with plans and schemes to achieve your goals. It will be easy! You already know where everything is! You can be a savior to the people of the town!

You pause and take stock of what you are about to do. Slowing down without moving, you take five deep breaths. Your mind clears a little, but you still feel strange.

"When in doubt, kick it out," you say aloud, remembering a soccer truism. But where is out?

Maybe you should go up and get Durno. He is probably still awake, and even though you don't want to admit it, he will have a good idea about what to do. However, you don't know how long Bram and Morphus will be at their meeting. They could come back at any moment so you need to make up your mind quickly!

If you decide to go down and sabotage the poison canisters,
turn to page 154.

If you choose to go back to warn Durno and get his advice,
turn to page 83.

Continued from page 10.

Sand Globe

I really miss the way the library smelled," you say. "It was sort of musty, but not in a sneezy way. It was comforting."

"How would you know? You were never there," Peter says.

"You either," Dresdale adds. "Glass houses and that sort of thing. But I know what you mean. The library was kind of old and dusty, but without the dust, if that makes any sense."

"I think they sell 'Old Library Smell' air fresheners like they do with 'New Car Smell,'" Peter yells.

"Why are you yelling?" you yell back to be heard above the now screeching wind, answering your own question in the process.

You move to the flap in the rear of the cart and open it. Bits of sand pepper your face and you close the flap. Wind makes the canvas of the cart rattle like rugs being pounded at a spring-cleaning. The cart stops.

"What happened?"

You open the front-end flap and look out, but you can't see anything except a wall of sand coming straight at you. Wind pushes you back into the cart.

"Where's the driver?!" Dresdale screams above the wail of

the wind.

"Gone!" you scream back.

"Close that flap!" Peter shouts in your ear. "Dres, get the other flap and tie it down."

You doubt that she heard him, but you move to stop the liquid current of sand pouring sideways into the cart. When you put your hands outside to grab the tie-ropes, you feel like your hands are being filed away by a pressure gun. It hurts but you do the job. You look over your shoulder and see that Dresdale and Peter have secured the back flap.

"What do we do now?" you shout.

"Wait it out," Dresdale shouts back.

This time, while waiting, the three of you don't share any stories. After an hour or so, you try peeking out again, and you don't see anything, but the sand blowing in is mixed with water.

Then the mud begins to drop from the sky in thick clumps onto the cart's flimsy canvas roof. It sags down like a water balloon, and the three of you scramble for the flaps...

They never find your bodies, or even the cart.

The End

Two Crows

Tat stares at you in disgust as you take half of the contents of the sack out and put it on the rough wooden table, but she does not stop you. You close the top of the sack and you are distracted by the feel of the rough cloth on your hands. Somehow that physical sensation of the roughness on your fingers is more real than the rest of the world, the rest of this situation.

"We gotta go!" Peter hisses.

Dresdale looks upset, but she moves out of the door without a backward glance. You follow Tat and Peter, and you glimpse behind you. You thought you might see a look of gratitude or relief on the woman's face, but, to your horror, you see disgust, rage, and fear combined in one look, directed at you, resulting in a large gobbet of mucus and spittle directed at you. Thankfully, she misses her target. Filled with guilt and shame, you quickly head out with your friends and Tat.

The journey back to your camp is tense, but you run into no one. Tat does not talk to you; she takes the bag of dried mushrooms and chews on one, seeming not to care if the three of you can keep up or not.

"That was some bad mojo," Dresdale says bitterly after you

get back to Noaaon and your camp in the blown-down trees. Tat brews tea from the herbs she found and gives it to Noaaon. "We stole that poor woman's food. Did you see how scared the baby was?"

"We only took half," you say in defense, feeling a growing ball of doubt and shame inside. "Besides, look at Noaaon; he seems better already and Tat has barely gotten any of that medicine down his throat."

"We still stole from and terrorized that woman and her baby."

"War is hell," Peter says, and you are not sure what that means in terms of your argument with Dresdale, but you all lapse into silence again.

You keep the first watch that night, while Tat works on Noaaon. You are tired and nervous, but the food gives you energy, and the thought of angry townspeople coming after you in the night keeps you alert.

"We go," Tat says from behind you. You did not hear her approach.

"What about Noaaon?" you ask.

"He walk. We go now."

That night is one of the worst of your life. Noaaon is barely conscious and stumbles blindly in the dark. You, Dresdale, and Peter help him as you sneak towards a hiding spot Tat knows about. She scouts ahead, and the night seems threatening and ominous. Strange calls from disturbed birds startle you, but once again, you see no one about.

You retch from exhaustion by the time you pull Noaaon's nearly lifeless body up a steep incline and into the shelter of a cave. Tat stays up all night, trying to help Noaaon, but the three of you fall asleep on the bare rock. Bile in your mouth tells you that you are still alive, you think as you fall asleep.

You spend the day in the coolness of the cave. Noaaon dies in the afternoon. Peter cries silently. Tears slide down his cheeks, leaving twin rivers of clarity down his dirt-darkened face. You are numb and don't know what you feel, exactly, but you know that it is not good.

"We're not going to just leave him here?" Dresdale says after Tat drags Noaaon's body out and places it on top of a boulder down from the cave.

"It is the way. He found. Eaten."

"Let's just go," you say. Tat has decided that it is impossible to make it to New Babel without Noaaon and with limited food. So, you are heading back from where you came. Your mission is a failure.

Two scouts find your small party, delirious and dying, two days from the border with the Forgotten People. Tat had finally abandoned you, after the three of you could not keep up. Your discoverers try to help you recover, but it is too late; you are too weak to continue on your journey...

The End

Sand Globe

W e're just being sensible," you say, justifying your decision. "If we got out there and ran out of food, who knows what might happen!"

"Right, Boy Scouts and all that. Let's get the food and move on."

You ride in the back of a cart pulled by low, flattened camels. Their tongues are forked like snakes and they taste the air frequently. The air is dry to your tongue, and you pull your robe tightly across your face to avoid the wind.

"What's up with this wind?" Peter shouts.

"It can't be good," Dresdale yells back.

You pass the time by talking about all the little things you miss.

"I always hated those hash brown morning things they always had at school—they were so greasy—but then, after a few years of eating them I really got to like them," Peter says with such wistful longing in his voice that you laugh.

"Don't remind me about those horrid lumps of undercooked potato and congealed grease. As a vegetarian I had to eat way too many of them. Gross," Dresdale says with a shudder. "You two could have the eggs and bacon and sausage. My choice was cereal, toast and those things. No protein except for milk."

Turn to page 5.

Continued from page 145.

Finger in the Clouds

On the fourth day of your enforced captivity, Marta becomes ill. When she wakes you up, you notice that her face is sweaty and pale. While making you breakfast, she suddenly clutches her side and slumps to the floor.

"Oh, nazul, nazul, nazul," she moans, pain making her voice thick. "Oh the pain, ohhh!"

Seeing a chance to both help her and get out of the apartment at the same time, you offer, "I'll go get someone! Just tell me where to go, and I'll get help!"

"Go tell my friend Luca, he is only two streets over, house with the purple steps. He will know what to do! Gods and nazul!" You help her into a chair and she writes a note on a scrap of paper, stopping to wince and whimper every few seconds.

You hurry out the door, pulling the orange robe around you as you leave the protection of the apartment and its garden for the first time in three days. It takes you a while to find Luca's house, but after backtracking a few times you find it and present the scrap to a small man with bandages on his thin hands. He picks at them absently while preparing a concoction from many stoppered bottles. It isn't until you are almost back to the apartment that you notice something pinned to the hem of your sleeve. It is a note.

You stop on the busy street and read it. Your heart freezes for a moment. The handwriting is familiar! The note is written in your father's neat but almost illegible script.

```
My Dearest Child,
Don't worry! Your mother and I are fine! We love
you and wish to see you, but we are having a hard
time communicating with the world outside of the
court. Be ready to come and meet with me when I
send  word,  and  be  discreet  and  extremely
cautious.  Don't  tell  anyone,  not  even  your
friends, or their lives may be in danger as well.
Your loving father,
Donald
```

Once again, your mind swirls. Your parents are alive!!! One of the metaphorical monkeys biting and perching on your back falls off, and you feel the other letting its grip loosen. Is it true, are they really safe? How did your father know where to find you? Why would telling your friends put their lives in danger? What does it all mean?

Continues in *The Golden Path, Volume III, Paying the Ferryman.*

Light in the Darkness

F ine," you decide. "We'll try and get the gerbil ball going. Dresdale, you have five minutes. If we can't at least get it fired up, we'll have to try and get out of here some other way."

"Great!"

"We may as well all get in the capsule," Peter offers, picking up his backpack and adjusting his head lamp. "It won't be long before the smoke fills this place."

You all clamber up the ladder to the loading platform. The hatch into the capsule is made of round, thick plates of riveted steel. You are reminded of pictures of rocket capsules. You know that they were designed to withstand the high heat of re-entry into the Earth's atmosphere, and you think that the same must be true in this case. You aren't sure if the extra plating makes you feel safer or not. It's sort of like needing a gun, often more dangerous than not having one.

"Look at this!" Dresdale shouts from inside. "It's a freakin' manual! Hot damn!"

"Just get it started," Peter says softly while strapping Neila into one of the four seats. Each seat has a six-point harness, and the two in front have control yokes and pedals. Dresdale takes the seat on the left, pilot-in-command, and you take the seat on the right.

Lights flash and a deep-throated roar from the engine shakes the craft.

"Do you want the good news or the bad news?" Dresdale asks earnestly as she flips switches while referring to the manual.

"Uh, bad, I guess," you mumble, not really sure if that is true.

"Well, this thing isn't quite as automatic as I was hoping, or wishing, really."

"What does that mean?"

"See those pedals below you?"

"Yeah."

"Well, your job is brakeman. Kind of like in the old days. I have to keep the capsule on track and moving forward. You have to make sure that we don't hit anything too hard. Or fall into a pool of magma or something."

"Great. What's the good news?"

"I got the capsule going!" Dresdale says with a big grin. Her teeth are a strange greenish-white from the glow of the switches and dials.

"I already knew that. I heard the engine."

"Doesn't make the news any less good."

You decide that is true, but choose not to say anything about it.

"I'm going to move us forward a bit, so keep your wits. Try the brakes out and see how they work before we really need them."

Dresdale leans forward against her harness, peering intently at the small screen in front of her while slowly moving a lever forward. You hear the engine respond, but the capsule stays still.

"Now to release the clutch...easy does it," she says.

The capsule shudders and jerks, and you are grateful for seat belts. You hear a loud but muffled sound of tearing and squealing metal. Looking out of the porthole, you see the ladder and platform mangled into a ball of twisted shapes. Dresdale doesn't seem to notice, she is so intent on the task of keeping the capsule moving forward.

"I'm going to hit the brakes," you warn. As soon as your foot pushes down, you are slammed into your restraints.

"A little lighter on the braking please," Peter says with false helpfulness. "Oh, and by the way, do you even know where we are supposed to be going?"

"Forward," Dredale replies. "Always moving forward, Peter, my friend. Always moving forward."

"What about the auto-pilot?"

"I haven't figured that out yet," Dresdale answers with a wild laugh. She is clearly having fun.

You move along the nearly featureless tube, but it is hard to tell how fast you are traveling, or how far you have gone. After awhile, your mind starts to wander. You are exhausted after the events of the day. The bitter disappointment of having your parents near, and then having them taken away again is too cruel. A few tears leak onto your cheeks and sneak into your mouth. The tears taste of smoke. It's too early to grow up, you think. But you have no choice.

"Brake! Hit the brake!!!" Peter yells. You snap out of your

self-pity and slam the brake pedal down in the nick of time. Before you is a wall of jumbled rock.

"Damn!" Dresdale swears in frustration. "Looks like a whole mountain came down into this one tiny spot."

"Not natural," sings Neila from the backseat. "Look at the walls."

"Whoooo! Those Radiant dudes are pretty hardcore characters," Peter says with a lot of awe and a little bit of fear. You look at the handprints burned into the smoothness of the rock walls and you feel the same way.

"Did they tear down the ceiling with their hands? What are they?"

"They are of the earth. They are energy. They are angry."

"Great. That's just great."

"Okay," you say, trying to sound confident. "Let's use this as an opportunity to get our bearings. Dres, study the manual and see what comes up. Peter, you and I'll check out the impasse and see if there is any way around it."

The capsule hatch hisses when it opens, and the cool, mineral smell of deep cave air fills your nose and lungs. You are thankful that the air is not sulfurous or poisonous or merely dead. The rocks shift underneath your feet as you scramble up the huge pile. Exhausted as you are, you realize there is nothing to do but shift as many rocks out of the way as possible.

"Don't look at the pile," Peter advises, seeing you staring at the wall of rocks. "It only makes it worse. Give me a hand with this one. I think that if both of us get on this side we can slide it forward."

Between the two of you, you manage to move only a fraction of the loose rocks. It looks hopeless. The thought of turning back fills you with dread and fear. It is just as likely, you suppose, that the Radiant Ones are lurking on the other side of the rock fall, but somehow the idea of going forward holds your mind in its grasp and won't let go.

"Thanks for trying, you guys," Dresdale says from the open hatch. "I think I might have a better method. Come check this thing out!"

You return into the capsule and watch in surprised wonder as Dresdale speaks into a command microphone. A nozzle extends from the front of the capsule and sprays a thick liquid on the rock pile.

"All right," Dresdale mutters, "just a bit of lubrication, and now we begin the extraction!"

A mechanical arm deploys from the top of the capsule and reaches forward to a large slab of rock wedged between the ceiling and the rest of the pile. A high pitch whine reaches you as you see the arm start to drill into the rock slab. The arm contracts and the rock follows it down to the side of the tunnel. While the mechanical arm seems to be designed precisely for this scenario, it's still a dangerous operation. You could be trapped forever by an avalanche of crushing rock.

"That's pretty slick, Dres."

"Yeah, not bad, huh? This thing is a monster. It looks like they thought of everything that could go wrong while cruising around inside the bowels of the Earth."

"What about fuel?" you ask. "How long do we have before we run out?"

"I don't think we need to worry about that for awhile," Dresdale answers. "This thing has its own nuclear power source. That is part of what gives us all this mass. This power plant could probably light up a small city and still have some to spare. Schliemann must have some pretty powerful friends to pull in resources like this."

You watch in silence as Dresdale carefully moves each rock out of the way. Peter tends to Neila, who appears to be sleeping. Thinking ahead to your mission into the caves, you take an inventory of food and water supplies. With everything on your mind, you're pleased that you actually remembered to pack any at all, but unfortunately you only brought enough for a day or two at the most. You have no idea how much Neila eats and drinks, but you suspect that it can't be much. But maybe glowing all the time really burns up calories. Who knows what the rules are here in the Inner Earth?

"We have 10 energy bars and five quarts of water, give or take. We'll need supplies pretty soon."

"Yeah, that's great," Peter mumbles, grabbing one of the energy bars. "I need a little energy right now. I'm exhausted."

"Hey Peter, will you take a look at this scrape on the back of my leg?" you ask. "I think it's bleeding again."

You wince in pain as he peels the fabric of your pants away from the partially scabbed wound. Jumping the fence and hiding in the shed of the abandoned factory seems like it happened a lifetime ago, and to a different person, rather than to you just a few hours ago.

"I hope that Harry and François are okay," you say as Peter

cleans your cut. The antiseptic stings, but somehow the pain feels good, grounding you in the here and now. He bandages it up with gauze and looks up at you for approval. "Nice job—thanks."

"I'm sure Harry and François are fine," Dresdale says, still intently working with the rock removal arm. "Those guys seem like they can handle themselves. But what happened to Maggie and Neila's friends?"

Your stomach clenches in despair and guilt. "I'm pretty sure the Radiant Ones got Neila's friends. I was so scared, I just ran. The Illuminated couldn't have outrun those flaming freaks with their little legs..."

Your eyes fill with tears, and no one says anything for quite a long time. You wish that you were back at school. Maybe all this really is just a bad dream.

"Did anyone see what happened to Maggie?" Dresdale asks.

"I don't know, she was with us for most of the time, and then suddenly she wasn't. Things got really confusing when the Radiant Ones showed up."

"I remember. How's the rock removal coming Dres?"

"Almost done! This thing is amazing."

With that, you hear a large crash from outside the capsule, and see the opening to the tube beyond grow wider as a large rock tumbles out of your way. The headlights from the capsule illuminate the tube: no burning evil ones stand ahead of you. You realize you've been holding your breath, and let it out slowly. You are safe—at least for now.

"Let's get out of here," Dresdale says, moving the capsule forward. The capsule's treads crunch over the remaining rocks like a centipede climbing a stick. It's bouncy and you struggle to get back into your harness.

Dresdale opens up the accelerator, and the capsule speeds along the featureless tube. You are exhausted, but you hang on in case you need to brake quickly. Peter's snoring and Neila's snuffling keep you awake. Jealousy at their state of blissful unconsciousness makes it all the more annoying. You eat an energy bar (Wild Berry!) and toss the wrapper at Peter's head, shooting for his open mouth. The wrapper hits him on the nose and bounces off; he doesn't even notice.

The tube twists and turns as you travel along at speed. It's like an amusement park ride, but slower. You can feel yourself going down and down into the heart of the Earth, and you try not to think about how far away the blue sky or the night stars are. What have you done to deserve this?

"See that up ahead?" Dresdale asks as she throttles back and the capsule slows to a crawl.

"Yeah, what is it?"

"I think it's a junction."

"Do you know which way to go?"

"I think so," she says with a touch of doubt. "Take a look at this map on the screen."

A schematic that looks like a tree's roots, but upside down, fills the small screen in front of you. Dresdale points to one of the 'roots' with her finger and taps the screen. You notice that all of the 'roots' are colored green, but right near her finger there is a thin red line connecting one 'root' to another.

"See how the larger pathways look organic? Well, I think that those are the actual volcanic tubes, which we have been traveling through. The straight red lines are artificial connectors between tubes. Look how this other one moves down and away from the main center of the ancient volcano. I think that is where we are supposed to go, but I'm not sure—it's pretty confusing."

"It sure is," you agree. "My head is pounding so hard right now that I can barely see. I trust your instincts, Dres."

"Fine, but don't blame me if we end up in the center of the volcano. Ancient or dead or not, it will be hot down there."

"I won't blame you. You're doing a great job. Thanks for helping me. You're awesome."

Dresdale doesn't respond, but her face breaks into a tired smile.

"Here goes nothing," she says, twisting the control yoke and spinning the capsule in place so that it faces a rough opening in the tube wall. You feel like the floor has dropped away as you careen down a rough-hewn shoot of rock. The Wild Berry bar gurgles in your stomach.

This is ten times worse than the monster roller coaster at the amusement park outside of Boston. You wish you were there right now, Gatekeepers and all, instead of facing the entrance to a volcano possibly surrounded by the Radiant Ones or forces even more evil.

The ride is short and rough. After ten minutes you enter another smoothbore tube. Dresdale calmly turns the capsule and continues on. You travel for about six more minutes and then she brings the capsule to a stop.

"I'm done!" she says, exhaling loudly and rubbing her head with her hands. "I have to get some sleep."

"Me too," you agree. You shift the seat back as far as it will go, and are pleasantly surprised that the whole thing goes horizontal. Your seat cradles you and you drift off while thinking about your parents...

You dream that you are in the middle of your trig test. Everything is flowing. You see the problems and you know the answers. It is as though your brain is on fire. Just as you are getting ready to hit submit on your test console, a flaming orange monster crashes through the wall of your classroom. Everyone scatters.

"There! Get that one!" A cruel voice commands. It's Dr. Schliemann, holding the reins to the Radiant One and coming right at you. The reins run to a silver collar around the burning figure's neck. Schliemann urges it on faster. You are frozen in fear. As it gets closer, The Radiant One opens its dark hole of a mouth and lets out a horrific scream that drowns out your own.

Your muffled screams jolt Peter awake. "Wake up! Wake up!" he shouts, shaking your shoulder. "It's just a dream. You're okay!" You struggle to shake off the nightmare as you become more fully conscious.

"Huh? What? Where are we?"

"Somewhere cold and dark. I was sleeping, too."

"Hopefully we're in the lower branch of the pathway into the Inner Earth, where they took your parents," Dresdale says with a yawn.

"Whoa, Ms. Dragon Breath, you might want to consider a breath mint," Peter teases.

"I would love one, you jerk, but I don't have any. Or a toothbrush."

"Well then, let me come to your assistance," he says with a flourish as he brings forth a small tin of mints. "Help yourself. Please. For all of our sakes."

"I'll have one too," you say, taking one of the small white mints and popping it into your mouth. The little bit of sugar makes you feel better immediately. "What's up with Neila?"

Peter's smile fades. "I don't know. He won't wake up. I don't want to shake him too hard. He looks so fragile."

"We're doing the best we can," Dresdale says, as if she was with a class of kindergartners doing a puppet project. "I'm sure he just needs more rest."

"Probably," agrees Peter, but he looks doubtful.

"Come on, let's get moving. I don't want my nightmare about the Radiant Ones to become a reality. The more progress we make the better."

Without the sun to give you clues about time, you fade into a sort of time warp, where things happen quickly and slowly at the same time. It doesn't bother you and you realize that you've adjusted well to this environment. You and Dresdale become a well synchronized team as you travel through the tubes. You encounter two more intersections, and Dresdale consults the 'root' map to find your direction.

"I'm not sure if this is it," she says as you enter another tube. "I wish they had signs or something."

"I think those burning guys would take them down," Peter

says with false seriousness. Dresdale gives a nervous laugh and continues driving.

You notice that the tube walls are getting wider and rougher until you lose sight of them in the darkness. You turn a sharp corner, entering a large cavern. A flat, black emptiness covers the floor of the cavern in front of you.

"Are we there yet?" Peter asks from the back. "Maybe I should take a turn driving?"

"Damn! Damn! Damn!" Dresdale curses. "This isn't where I thought we were. Sorry, guys, I don't know where we are."

"Don't worry about it," you say soothingly, even though you are in fact worried about it. "At least we aren't in the heart of a volcano."

The three of you fade into silence, staring out across the different levels of darkness. You feel the weight of the rock above pushing down on your consciousness. You squirm at the thought of it crushing you beneath its weight.

"Let's check it out," you say as a way of dealing with your fear and claustrophobia.

"I'll stay here with Neila," Peter says. He looks worried. "I still can't rouse him and his glow seems to be lessened."

"You have no idea what his natural patterns are," Dresdale says reasonably. "Maybe this is just a natural phase he goes through sometimes."

"He said he was ill!" Peter snaps. "Weren't you listening?"

"I think I have been a little preoccupied, Peter—geez. Come on, let's get out of this thing."

You use the emergency rope ladder to climb down from the capsule. The sandy ground is white under the illumination from your headlamps. It is disturbed in places, but you can't tell from what. There aren't any footprints, but you get the feeling that someone, or something, has been here.

Moving towards the blackness and away from the gerbil ball, you immediately get relief. You see a broad lake that is quite still. You hear water dripping, but you don't see any ripples in the light from your headlamp. Dresdale approaches the edge of the water and kneels down. She pauses, looks back at you and shrugs as if to say "well, here goes...," then puts her scooped hand into the blackness, bringing a handful of the liquid to her lips.

"It tastes fresh!" she says, relieved. "We can fill our bottles here! Man, I was getting worried."

You remain suspicious. "You sure we won't get sick from it? What if it has bacteria or something else?"

"We don't have much choice," she explains. "Besides, I'll bet that by the time any water makes it down here, it will have been filtered by the earth above us."

"I'll buy that," you agree. "But how do we get across this lake? If that is what we want to do."

"I don't think we can. Maybe there is something else about water travel in the manual, but I doubt this vehicle can float for long. I can't even see to the other side of this lake. Right now our best bet is to retrace our tracks and try to figure out where we went wrong."

"Guys! Come here! Neila's awake! He knows where we are!!" You're amazed to learn that Peter and Neila are unscathed. "Peter! You're okay!"

You look at Dresdale to see her expression, but you are blinded by the glare of the headlamp in your eyes. "Okay, then, let's find out what they know." As you turn away, you see ripples spreading across the lake.

By the time you make it back to the vehicle, Peter and Neila have descended the ladder and are headed toward you. "He just snapped awake! When he looked out of the portholes, he said he knows where we are!"

"Is true," Neila says in his gentle, high-pitched voice. "We are at the Lake of Dreams. Dangerous, but close. Do not go in. Do not swim!!"

"Where are we, exactly?" Dresdale asks.

"The Lake of Dreams," Neila answers with a shudder. "Very dangerous. Very holy. There is a path up. We must go."

"Go where?"

"Up, up to the red. Not my home. But close. Close. I have been here. Very dangerous."

"What's dangerous? Dresdale drank some of the lake water. Will she be alright?"

"Not the water danger. What is in water. We must go."

"Come on!" Peter whines. "You heard Neila! We're almost there!"

"Just hold on, Peter. I'm not sure what has gotten into you, but we need to get our stuff."

Dresdale packs quickly, tucking the capsule's manual into her backpack before leaving the small cabin. It has been a shelter for your group, and you feel sad to leave it.

"No lock, no keys," Dresdale explains, closing the hatch and climbing down. "Hopefully no one will get in and mess around."

"Do you think we'll be coming back?" you ask.

"I hope so," she answers. "It's the only way back home that

I know of."

You don't answer, but you think about the Radiant Ones and the fact that the last time you saw them, they were between you and the exit from Carlsbad Caverns. You have a feeling you won't be coming back this way, but sometimes your feelings are wrong. But...what about your parents?

Peter rigged his backpack to carry Neila inside it. His glowing head and shoulders stick out. Neila has his arms wrapped tightly around Peter's neck.

"The path is back across the wide open space, near where the cavern opens up," Peter says as he leads you away from the lake. "It should be like an old tower staircase."

"Lead on, MacDuff!"

With Neila's help, Peter finds the path upwards and away from the Lake of Dreams. What is so dangerous about the place? You think about the ripples and what might have caused them. Soon all thoughts are wiped from you except for the chore of putting one foot in front of the other as you climb a stone staircase the leads on and on. It seems to go nowhere.

"How far does this thing go?" Dresdale asks after you have been climbing for a long while. "This is more of a workout than I'd planned on."

"Look, Dres, I don't know. Keep quiet, Neila's asleep," Peter says before turning and tromping up the stone staircase.

Turn to page 103.

Recap of your story so far from *The Golden Path, Vol. 1, Into the Hollow Earth*.

Having entered the inner world through the North Pole route, you and your friends meet the Lemurians for the first time. Your rejection of the Truth Enlightenment Ritual, a dangerous but high honor, creates tension with Sublimas-Chaeko, the leader of the band of Lemurians, resulting in your having to leave the resources and safety of their compound. Durno, your Lemurian guide, helps you, Peter, Rimy, and Dresdale to head for the wilderness in pursuit of your parents. You fear that they might be dead, or, even worse, that they might be traitors! You travel for days before coming to a deserted village...

From *Volume I, Into the Hollow Earth*, p. 68

"There should be smoke. From cookfires," Durno states tersely. "Its absence makes me keen."

He takes off at a trot, and the four of you try to follow. Your mountain trail feeds into a road paved with cobblestones. Durno is now far ahead, running.

You finally reach the Arcata city gates. Durno stands quietly, tears streaming down his face.

"There has been an evacuation," he whispers. "This cannot be good."

"I think I hear someone crying," Dresdale says. She darts forward, looking.

You follow and turn a corner on to a town square. A young girl, covered in soot, runs toward you, sobbing.

"What is she saying?" you ask. She jumps into Durno's grasp and throws her small arms around him.

Durno listens as the young girl speaks haltingly.

He looks slowly to you as she speaks.

"Strangers came. They ordered the men into the woods. She thinks they were shot. And the women and children were forced to march to the capital."

Durno asks a few questions.

"She says some of the strangers were your people, from the outer Earth," he continues.

You hold out a photo of your mom and dad in your wallet.

"Did you see these people?" you ask the girl.

"Yes, they were in the lead," Durno translates.

Plaster explodes above your head. Your cheek is a small flower of pain. Durno lies at your feet. He is not moving.

"Come on! Grab him, we need to get out of here!"

Your story continues...

Under Cover

Help me grab his legs!"

"Get his head, oh god, I hope he's okay!"

"Get down, and get under cover," you yell.

Rimy grabs your hand and pulls you to the safety of a deserted doorway. Peter and Dresdale drag Durno's unmoving body into the house. It is a mess inside. Tables and chairs have been upended, and papers and broken dishes litter the floor, but it is a haven compared to being outside and under fire.

"He's breathing!" Peter shouts.

"Stop shouting, we're indoors!" Dresdale yells back.

Durno moans pitifully once and then screams.

"Who shot at us?" you ask.

"Someone who is not our friend, or who was scared. That girl said they took the men away. Maybe they didn't get them all," Rimy says as he inspects Durno's body for wounds. "Here it is. Dresdale, find some cloth, preferably clean, and tie it around his leg. Peter, you peek outside and see what you can."

"Is it bad?" you ask.

"I think it may have come out the other side of his leg," Rimy explains, tying the cloth, "and the fall to the street was what knocked him unconscious. Look! His eyes are opening. We have to get out of here."

"Looks clear out the front and the back doors, but I vote for the back," Peter says, inching back from the open front door. "I never caught sight of the sniper."

You carry Durno out the back door, worrying about getting shot at any moment. It is a horrible feeling and it lasts until you are out of the village and into the relative safety of the woods. Durno regains consciousness, but is unable to walk with the wound to his leg. You and your friends stumble through the towering red trees, until you find a hollow created by rocks and fallen trunks.

You spend the day looking for food and caring for Durno. Neither endeavor results in much success. All you manage to find are some roots and nuts. There is no animal life nearby.

"He needs real help," Dresdale declares after looking at Durno. "I think he has a fever. I don't know if Lemurians are the same as humans, but we look a lot alike, and he seems to be fighting an infection. Where can we find a doctor?"

"Who knows? We did what we could," Rimy replies, "and right now, that will have to do."

"But my parents were in that town! Only a little while ago. We have to go after them!"

"We can't leave a wounded friend; that is not the way any of us would want to be treated," Rimy says tiredly.

"Why don't some of us take him to a doctor, or whatever they have here, and the others will go after my parents?"

"Haven't you ever seen one of those old-time horror movies? Never split up! Especially if you're all in swimsuits," Peter says, trying to lighten the tone of the conversation.

"We're not in a horror movie," you explain. "This is real life."

"So far it seems about par for the course, now all we need is some sort of monster," Dresdale says as if pointing out a theme in English class. "You know, a nice monster who only eats annoying boys."

"You better not be talking about me," Peter warns, "'cause I'm almost a man."

"The key word being 'almost'," Dresdale retorts.

"My parents are getting farther and farther away as we speak," you interrupt, "and if we don't go after them now, it may be too late."

If you agree with Rimy and keep the group together until Durno is taken care of, turn to page 179.

If you choose to send two people with Durno to find medical help, and go with another in search of your parents, turn to page 177.

Recap of your story so far from *The Golden Path, Vol. 1, Into the Hollow Earth.*

Taking your archaeologist parents' flying skimmer, you and your friends flew to Carlsbad, New Mexico, to meet the mysterious "Uncle" Harry, who was not really your uncle. Instead he was a member of FFA, an insurgent group. Harry introduced you to Neila, one of the Illuminated; a being who shines with internal light. On a dual purpose mission to transport Neila and his companions home and rescue your parents, everything goes wrong as the Radiant Ones, burning guardians of the volcanic tube network, exact their revenge on trespassers. Neila is too weak to transport himself home via the crystal network, but he has told you that your parents have been taken inside of the Earth.

From *Volume I, Into the Hollow Earth*, p. 170

You see the hated Gatekeepers, armed with rifles, rush toward the glowing figure of a Radiant One standing in the ruins of the lab buildings.

"Fire!" yells the Gatekeeper in charge. The Gatekeepers fire their rifles at once. Without seeming to notice the effect of bullets ripping into its body, the Radiant One turns to the uniformed Gatekeepers. In three swift moves, it grabs a Gatekeeper, picks him up, and throws his burning body at the others.

"Keep moving!" Peter yells as he grabs your arm. Dresdale is with him, and she is cradling Neila in her arms like a child.

"Where?!"

"Away from these burning freaks!" he shouts as he pulls you into a thick wall of smoke. Choking on the fumes, you rush forward, banging your knees and shins, but making good time.

"Neila says his transport site is only a little farther on. If we can get him there he can contact the Inner Earth people and warn them."

The noise of the battle raging behind you recedes as you travel deeper into the cave system. You are in shock. Your parents were in the building that was burning. That was what Maggie told you.

"Where's Maggie?!"

"I don't know," Dresdale says, turning to look at you. "Do you know where Neila's friends are?"

A spasm of guilt makes you heart hurt. "I think they're dead. One of the burning things caught them."

"Oh."

"Little ways," Neila whispers to Peter. "I will show."

Neila stands and moves toward a massive stalagmite in the center of the small cave. It is much taller than the small being. Neila begins to sing, and then he reaches out his glowing hand and touches the crystal stalagmite. It begins to glow and pulse the same color as Neila. He sways and gives a soft moan.

"Much news," Neila says, stepping away from the crystal.

The glow stops. Neila looks at you. "Child of the Child, your parents have been taken in."

"What? What are you talking about?" you ask, frightened at being called 'Child of the Child.'

"The Radiant Ones were waked by our passage to the inner world. Parents no longer here. You come inside as well. It is the only way. The Radiant Ones is death. I am too weak to travel by crystal. We will have to take the path that has been opened."

"I think I hear them coming," Peter whispers. Dresdale tugs at your sleeve.

"Come on, let's go," you say, setting aside your exhaustion and fear.

Your story continues...

Gerbil Ball Pachinko

You don't know what to feel. A moment ago you thought your parents had been burned alive, now Neila, one of the glowing beings called The Illuminated, tells you that they have been taken inside the Earth. A rippling wave of black smoke snaps you into the present. Even Neila's glowing face is hidden by the smoke from the fires of the Radiant Ones.

"Let's follow Neila," you say. "If we go back through the smoke, we'll die."

"Here, Neila, I'll carry you," Peter says gently to the small being. Neila puts his arms around Peter's neck like a child, and Peter lifts and walks deeper into the caves, aglow in Neila's soft blue light.

"We can't just leave Maggie and the others!" Dresdale protests, coughing.

"We don't have a choice. Even if we could make it through the smoke, which we can't, we'd be going right toward the Radiant Ones, and meeting them once was more than enough for me! Come on!"

"Just promise me we'll come back and look for them if we can!"

"I promise already!"

You take Dresdale's hand and pull her after you. Peter and Neila are moving towards a large, dark hole.

"Neila!" you shout, "where are we going?"

Peter turns his head and you can see him glaring at you by Neila's illumination. He makes an exaggerated shushing motion and beckons you onward.

"Neila says we should cut through this gap and then we'll be near the volcanic tube system that Schliemann was using."

"Then what?"

"I don't know. Let's just keep moving for right now. The farther I can get from those burning men the better."

"Amen on that!"

Once through the hole, you enter a tubular cave complex. No smoke is visible, but you can't get the burning smell out of your nose. Your headlamps show a passageway that looks well-used. Parts of it are poured-concrete pathways. You see light fixtures, but none of them are on. You assume the power supply was hit by the fires.

"Look at the damage they did!" Dresdale fumes in outrage, pointing her light at a spot near the ceiling, denuded of all natural formations to make way for a lighting stand. "Your parents would never have allowed this! What were they doing?"

"They must have been in a hurry," you reply. "They didn't even wait for the floor to fully dry before using it." You indicate the portion of the floor with permanent tread marks from the time it was still wet cement.

"What was the special hurry?" Dresdale wonders, caught for a moment in the mystery.

"They wanted to get your parents inside. Or maybe they

wanted to get inside anyway, but the first people they sent through were your parents," Peter says with logical certainty. You feel sick.

The question remains, who were they?

"Whatever it is, we may as well go farther in and see what they were up to."

You follow the cement path deeper into the cave. The ceiling of the cavern lowers, and the mass of cables and tubes above your head comes closer. No one says anything. You must be in one of the volcanic tubes. The walls become smoother and less jagged. Eventually you enter a section that has been expanded.

"I think this is it," Peter says in a whisper. "Look over there!"

You turn to see a series of ashen shadows on the walls of the cave. The shadows are of people cowering in fear. You think they are the workers in the lab, transformed into afterimages of ash on a cave wall. You shudder and feel ill. It is like the pictures of Hiroshima, the site of the first atomic bomb attack on people, Japan 1945.

"Why doesn't it smell like smoke?"

"I don't know! You're really horrible sometimes, Dres!" Peter snaps.

Neila's singing voice echoes sharply in the confined space of the tube. "They had time. Time to eat. They take it all when they have time. They leave no sign but ash. They have been burned. Cremated."

"Do you think this is what they were working on?" Peter asks, pointing at the round, hulking shape taking up much of the area in the expanded tube. Metallic and plastic, it looks like a giant ball.

"Of course, dumbo," Dresdale says nastily. "What else is there?"

"Cut it out, you two! It is not helpful hearing you bicker," you say, inspecting the strange vehicle or capsule that Schliemann was working on. A rolling ladder with a platform stands next to an open hatch. Overall the thing is round, with hooks and treads covering it from top to bottom. A tread with iron hooks runs right through the split windshield. In the rear of the vehicle, there are inverted black cones that make you think of speakers for a sound system.

"Neila, you know more about this than the rest of us. What can you tell us?"

"No, not much. Only pass this way once. Long ago. Is passage to the inner world. I travel...differently before. Others have done so. Very dangerous. Radiant Ones. Lots of walking. Climbing. Crawling. Spiders."

"Neila?" Peter whispers so quietly that you can barely hear him. "If we needed to take the route you are talking about, could you show us the way?"

"What are you suggesting?" Dresdale demands. "Do you really think we should try and hike, or crawl, into the center of the Earth? You're nuts."

"What do you want to do?" Peter retorts. "Drive some sort of glorified gerbil ball into an active volcano? You're the one who's nuts. Not me."

"Please. The smoke," Neila sighs. "It hurts."

You hadn't noticed it while inspecting Schliemann's toy, or

gerbil ball, as Dresdale characterized it, but the tube is getting smokier and smokier. Standing still is no longer an option.

"I bet the capsule is programmed. We can probably just sit back and enjoy the ride while it follows the set course."

"I don't know," you say, aware that Neila is coughing deeply. You hope that the Radiant Ones aren't coming for you. "I doubt it's as simple as that. This thing looks a lot more complicated than the flyer."

"Yeah, the flyer. We did alright with that, didn't we? Look, we don't have time to sit around here. We need to decide. Neila is about to pass out, and I'm not far behind. Can't we at least give it a try?" Peter begs.

If you choose to take the gerbil ball, Schliemann's volcanic tube transport capsule, turn to page 13.

If you decide to head deeper into the cave complex with Neila as your guide, turn to page 44. Remember, he is ill and failing.

"...Thicker Than Thieves."

If they're in New Babel, we won't have to waste our time looking in caves for mystic answers. We need to use the best information that we can."

"Very well," Prince Torgan says. He looks disappointed. "I will do my best to see that you succeed, Emerald Warrior. If you are fated to meet Orana, there is nothing you can do to prevent it."

You leave in the morning, and you learn the news at the last minute.

"What do you mean you're not coming?" you ask Durno.

"Not enough room in the hiding spot. We three will go back. We are needed there."

"Good luck," you say, gamely, but you feel the fear of being on your own.

The method of smuggling you into Agartha is both effective and smelly. A truck loaded with manure gets few inspections, especially at the bottom of the pile. You, Peter and Dresdale spend three days cramped in a box the size of half a car. There is no room to stand, but you have fresh air piped in, food and water.

Luckily, you can crawl out of the bottom of the truck for short breaks, but most of the time you are stuck inside.

"This stinks," Peter says for the hundredth time.

"Ha, ha, please come up with a new one," Dresdale says tiredly.

You are delivered to a farm on the edges of New Babel. Unfortunately, you are not allowed to get a glimpse of the city. Your driver tells Dresdale of its amazing tower that pierces the sky like a black spike. He hurries you to a door on the side of a barn and gives you a slap on the back as a farewell. The barn door slams behind you, and all is dark.

"Welcome to New Babel, Emerald Warrior, Child of the Child, if you know what that means," a voice says from the darkness. It is a melodious, male voice with a faint accent. "We have waited a long time to meet you."

"Who are you?" you ask, hoping that you are not guessing correctly. "We need help finding my parents, Dianna and Donald Torman. Can you help us?"

"Of course I will help you, Child of the Child, for I am your grandfather; I am Sceptus," the voice says as a red light flashes on. You are facing an old man dressed in robes of gold and black. He holds a staff with a glowing red crystal hand. It is the source of the illumination, and it makes everyone look like the undead.

"It was a trap, damn! I knew it!" Peter says as three men in black and gold grab you and your friends. "Must have been the driver!"

"Do not struggle. I am not the enemy. All that the Lemurians have told you is lies. Lies told by those who eat the life force of the dead. Vampires. The unclean. I will educate you."

"What about my parents?!"

"My daughter, Dianna, and your father are quite well. You will see, I am not an evil man. Far from it—I am family. Blood is thicker than thieves."

The End

All Wrapped Up

Hey Neila, I think we should go by the route you actually know. You're sure you can find the way?" you ask.

"Dangerous, yes," he replies, before collapsing with a coughing fit. After it passes, he wipes his small mouth and licks his lips. You notice that his tongue glows amidst his sharp teeth. Peter picks him up gently.

"Show us the way, friend," Peter says, stifling a cough of his own in the smoky air. Neila points his little hand down the tunnel. The four of you make your way towards the route to the inner world. Fresher air gives you more strength and improves the visibility provided by your headlamps and by Neila's shining form—his illumination.

You travel through caves and caverns; some are enormous, while others are more like thin ribbons of space between a world of crushing rock. Taking deep breaths and remembering the Radiant Ones behind you keeps you motivated to continue amidst a rising sense of claustrophobia.

"Boy, I wish we could have more time to really explore some of these caverns instead of just rushing through them," Dresdale says as you pass under a dripping roof covered in soda straw formations. Neila's light makes them glow with a pulsing radiance that is stunning.

Occasionally you have to use your ropes to get up or down some tricky obstacles, but nothing is too technical to prevent you from advancing.

"Wait!" Neila says after you reach the sandy floor of a dark grotto of bulbous rock. This descent was one of the more difficult ones, and you hope deeply that you will not have to go back up it. "Not on path, Child of the Child!"

You look around, but since you were depending on Neila to show you the way, you don't really know what to look for in terms of how you have gone wrong. The sandy floor has weird holes spaced evenly in two separate lines, and chunky heaps of tangled gray ropes. It smells of rot and musk.

"Looks like someone has been here before," Peter says. "So we're not too far off the mark. We'll just have to backtrack a bit."

"Come on," Dresdale says, "the climb back up isn't going to get shorter if we wait around."

You prepare to make the climb, chagrined.

"What was that?!" you say, startled by a loud chittering sound from above you. It sounds like bacon being fried by a jackhammer.

Neila's eyes go wide, and he is about to yell something when a clump of gray rope covers his whole head in a moist, clinging mass.

"What the…?"

Before you can move, you feel something wet and heavy hit your head. You bring your hands up and scrape enough of the sticky mass away from you face so that you can see and breathe.

You look up.

Poised above, hanging from a thread that travels into the darkness is a creature that is all mouth and legs. It looks as large as a car. Two large fangs clench and gnash, while two legs reach back to grab more silk from the spinnerets.

After the first bite, you feel no more pain, even as your body starts to liquefy.

The End

Continued from page 131.

Finger in the Clouds

"Yeah, it is pretty crazy looking," you agree. I mean, look at those flying lizards! They're almost like birds, but not quite. The way they fly doesn't make sense to the eye, it's like they're being pulled by strings into the air and then dropped down again almost randomly."

You sleep that night within the shelter of the cave hideout and your dreams are of farmhouses, babies and the most wonderful mushroom dinner. Then someone tells you that the mushrooms aren't mushrooms but rather the souls of children. You wake scared and sweaty.

The next day, Tat and Noaaon take you over two mountain ridges and you get your first glimpse of New Babel. It is a shocking scene to you after your time inside this world of red light and red desert. Everything is steel or glass, mostly green. Huge dirigibles hang over the city like balloons at a kid's birthday party, but these balloons are drab in color, and you think they may have guns or missiles or something hanging from their command capsules.

Gigantic tractors plow fields of red dirt, while harvesters gather in whole fields of greenery in one gulp. Smoke billows into the sky from factories, obscuring the far side of the city

from your view, but it does not obscure the most prominent feature of the city. A tower reaches up into the sky, like a finger thrust out of the sand by a person who has been buried and is reaching for freedom. It spirals high above the anchored dirigibles, dark and intimidating.

"They look busy," Peter observes at your lookout point above the valley below.

"Busy getting ready for war," Dresdale agrees. "You can almost feel the aggression emanating from this place. Look at those factories, and those huge trucks bringing stuff back and forth. What are they using for fuel? Tat told me there is no oil on the inside of the Earth, or at least, very little. Energy, fresh water, and food have always been scarce here, which has kept

the technological level from advancing on the strength of the internal combustion engine and irrigated farming."

"I would say they have worked those problems out," you say.

"No kidding, that is one serious operation down there."

Tat smiles for the first time as she hurries you along after your rest break. You guess that she is glad to be getting rid of you. The meeting with your contact in New Babel is near, and you are eager to move away from the sternness and dourness of Tat and Noaaon. Eager to step out of your role as a thief.

Tat brings out four orange robes from her pack and hands one to each of you and keeps one for herself. Noaaon doesn't get one. It is light and soft, and has a hood to cover your head.

She leads you into a small town on the deep outskirts of New Babel. You pass a number of other people, but they pay you no mind as they are similarly dressed. She leads you to shed behind what looks like an unused warehouse or other storage building and motions you inside the dark doorway with an urgent waving of her hand.

"Welcome, Child of the Child!" a woman says to you in oddly accented English as soon as you enter. She rushes towards you in a swirl of orange cloth and presses something into your hand. It is a perfect blue crystal, shaped into the form of a rod. It glows with an internal light and feels heavy for its size in your hand. An electric thrill rushes into you, and you feel as if you are about to faint.

"It was your great-grandfather's, may he have his peace! You are the one, the one to free us from the yoke of the usurper!"

"What are you talking about?" you mumble, reeling from the waves of warmth emanating from the rod. "What do you mean?"

"I go now," Tat says, and as is her wont, she slips out of the warehouse door without pausing or saying anything else.

"Yeah, thanks, great to get to know you and all that," Peter says with sarcasm and truth at the same time.

"We wouldn't have made it without her," you remind him.

"Maybe that would have been better."

"Do you know where my parents are?" you ask the woman in the same orange robes as you, changing the subject and getting to the reason for your coming. "What is your name?"

"I am Marta," she says, rather shyly. "Your parents are with the emperor in the tower."

"The Tower of New Babel?" Dresdale asks with a laugh.

"Of course," Marta replies, "it was built when the old was destroyed, long ago. We are working to get in touch with your parents, but it is hard. They are under constant guard. Only when there are public ceremonies are they allowed where the people can see them, and even then it is hard, so hard to get in contact."

Turn to page 143.

Recap of your story so far from *The Golden Path, Vol. 1, Into the Hollow Earth.*

After being expelled from the Alstone School for stealing a pottery shard, you return home to find your parents are missing and your mom's dog, Tito, dead in your garage. You and your friends Peter and Dresdale take your parents' flyer and head to Carlsbad, New Mexico, after receiving an ominous email from your mother telling you to meet your Uncle Harry there. However, after spending a day hiding under a willow tree by a river, waiting for night, you encounter a person, or being, in a town filled with only the burned shadows of its previous inhabitants, mere shadows on the walls...

From *Volume I, Into the Hollow Earth*, p. 102

"What are you talking about?" Your head is spinning. *Maybe he is just a crazy. Maybe he is here to lead you astray. Or maybe this is just a bad dream.*

But then how did he know who you were? How did he know about your parents?

"The Inner Earth is like a Mobius strip, once on it, you never get off...unless you break the strip."

"What are you talking about? "Inner Earth" is just out of the comic books of years ago. It's a fable, a kid's story."

"If that is what you think, then leave! You'll never find your parents— little good it will do anyway if you do." He seems to be shrinking, becoming less and less human, more concept than reality.

"There are many ways into the Inner Earth. Carlsbad Caverns is only one way. And it is a dangerous way. The Radiant Ones control one of the secret entrance gates. They kill all who know or try to find the path. They

followed me and my colleagues here to this simple town and destroyed it in an orgy of hate.

"My parents. How long? Why? Where now?" you can barely speak.

"Seek them in the Inner Earth. But Carlsbad is clogged now. It has drawn too much attention to itself. Big Sur is the place now. Few know of that entrance." He gives a sudden pause.

"That is all I can tell you. I must go."

He fades to nothing, like so much wood smoke in open air.

You turn around and run as fast as you can back to Dresdale and Peter.

Your story continues...

On the Road

You run as fast as you can back to the river. Peter and
Dresdale are getting the flyer ready for the night's flight to
Carlsbad.

"Hey, are you okay?" Peter asks, while you struggle to catch
your breath.

"No!" you gasp. "We have to get out of here!"

"Whoa, what just happened? I thought it was pretty empty
country out here."

"There was this man," you say. "He had a gun, and then he
told me to go to Big Sur and that the Radiant Ones were
coming back. They killed everyone!"

"Killed?! What are you talking about?" Dresdale asks, her
eyes big. "Where did you go?"

"Just over across the fields and over a small hill. There's a
town there, or the used to be a town there. Most of the buildings have been burned down. He said they came out of the
ground, and that they burned so hot they turned people into
ash-shadows!"

"Do you want me to check it out?" Peter asks, sounding
braver than he looks.

"No, I don't think that's a good idea. He said they would

be back. He said Carlsbad was a trap, and that we had to go to Big Sur. Then he disappeared!"

Peter looks at Dresdale and raises his eyebrows in a way that implies: "Our friend has had a difficult time, and maybe is going a little crazy."

"I'm not crazy!" you exclaim.

"Never said you were," Peter replies calmly, with the soothing voice of a parent helping a toddler through a tantrum. "Regardless of what just happened, we should get going. It will be dark soon; we have to move on."

"Come on, help me with the tarp," Dresdale says.

"First, supposing you did meet this guy, how are we supposed to get to Big Sur?" Peter asks as he pilots the flyer above the treetops. "Our codes only allow us to fly to Carlsbad."

"We'll just have to risk it," you say.

"That sounds smart," Dresdale says mockingly. "Anyway, where in Big Sur are we supposed to go? It's a big area."

"I don't know, he didn't say where. I thought it's a town."

"Nope, an area. Kind of big, like I said."

"Listen, Dres, I don't know why you are giving me a hard time, but a dude just had a shotgun pointing at my head in a town full of dead people's shadows. I'm a little stressed and I don't need the aggravation right now."

"Hey guys," Peter interrupts suddenly. "Something weird is going on."

"Add it to the list," you mutter bitterly.

"Hey, I'm sorry," Dresdale says. "I'm just scared."

"Yeah, yeah, we're all scared," Peter agrees, "but right now I'm trying to figure out how we got approval to fly to California."

"What do you mean?"

"The codes have been downloaded into the flyer."

"How do you know?"

"Look," Peter says, pointing at the small dashboard.

You see the small schematic map of your route. Peter had put in Big Sur as the destination, and instead of it flashing a baleful red of denial, it glowed with the green of acceptance.

"At least we won't have to fly by the seat of our pants on manual mode!" Dresdale says with such forced cheerfulness that you glare at her. "Not that I don't trust you, Peter, but your pants are a bit dirty for flying."

"Ha, ha, very funny. I haven't been able to get my laundry done recently, so go ahead, laugh at my expense, but it doesn't change the fact that someone added the codes. It just all seems too convenient. We stop randomly somewhere and you meet a guy who knows your parents and then we suddenly have the codes that allow us to get to Big Sur."

"What else should we do?" you ask. "You weren't there. It was spooky. The burned buildings, the guy disappearing. I think he was really trying to warn us. I think he knew something bad was waiting for us in Carlsbad."

"Fine, we'll go to Cali, but I think it's strange."

"Of course it's strange!" Dresdale says, exasperated. "This whole thing doesn't make any sense. Just fly this crate!"

The three of you pass several hours in silence, caught in endless loops of 'what if' and 'what will be' inside your heads. You wonder where your parents are and if they are okay. Below, the landscape slowly changes as you zoom across the flatness of the heartland and towards the Rocky Mountains. In the clear fall air, squares and triangles of human land boundaries are visible in the moonlight. Luminescent white snow tops the highest peaks in the distance.

"Listen, Peter, I know that you are just trying to be careful," Dresdale says, long after you assumed she had fallen asleep. Her voice is thick with the thoughts of late night. "And I know it sounds strange coming from me, because I like to plan and stuff, but we need to keep going, even if it seems crazy."

"Maybe. We'll see," Peter demurs.

You spend the next day in the surreal landscape of the Canyonlands of Utah. With above-average rainfall over the last thirty years, the landscape is a contrast of deep greens and the rich reds of the mushroom-shaped walls of once-flowing rock. You stash the flyer in a thick copse of cottonwoods and survey the Green River.

Peter snores underneath the shade of the flyer while you talk with Dresdale about Big Sur and your encounter with the man back in the burned-down town. Your head feels thick and stuffy, and you wonder if you are coming down with a cold. Everything feels detached, as if your cord to reality had been cut. Even the coolness of the water on your face as you wash it in the river feels too wet, too cold, too distant to be real.

"I could live in a place like this," Peter says from behind, startling you without making you jump.

"I don't know," you answer, playing your part. "Even with the greenery, you can tell this is still a desert. Everything feels wrong. Fake somehow."

"Not sure I'm pickin' up what you're layin' down, but I do want to know what you guys have done for food," Peter says, clearly not wanting to get into a philosophical discussion at this time. "I'm starving," he adds for emphasis.

By the time you are finished with lunch, you realize that you have minimal food supplies left for the rest of your journey.

"I don't think I want to risk going into town," Dresdale says, looking at an empty bag of dried fruit. "Even though I would love a really good salad for dinner, and not more dried-out stuff."

"Not sure I would risk anything for a salad, but I agree," Peter says. "We should make it to Big Sur by tomorrow. Assuming our codes are still good..."

"Yeah, well, we have some sardines, a few pieces of jerky, and some crackers, but that's about it."

"We'll just have to make do," Dresdale says. "But I claim the crackers. You meat-eaters can have the other stuff."

You leave the Canyonlands as the sun is setting, the glare in your eyes making you squint. A few tears fall out of your tightly pressed eyes. Peter and Dresdale don't say anything so you are not sure if they noticed or not. During the night you had heard Peter crying out, but by the time you got out of your sleeping bag to check on him he was sleeping soundly.

"So, where are we going, exactly?" Dresdale asks once you are flying safely in the darkness of night.

"Well, I just took a look at where the access codes allow us to go, and they are cleared for us heading all the way to the coast," Peter explains as he pilots the flyer and pulls up your route on the map screen. "Somewhere north of where Monterey used to be, about 30 miles or so. It looks kind of isolated on the map. I'm not sure who we'll be able to meet there."

"Whom we'll be able to meet," Dresdale corrects absent-mindedly.

"Thanks, Teach!"

Flying over the Sierra Mountains under moonlight is beautiful, but the feeling of unreality has not left you, and it all seems to slide past you like dreams fading in the morning sun. Over and over again you replay the scene at your house. The email from your mom. Tito, dead on the floor. The conversation with Mr. Billings. The man with the shotgun. It all bounces around inside you and doesn't allow you any peace. Even when you sleep it all combines into one big ball of sticky anxiety that makes you want to scream and vomit all at the same time.

"We'll be there shortly," Peter says. "Please fasten your seat belts, but don't complain about the cancellation of the in-flight meal, just pull your belts tighter!"

"It's not getting any funnier, you know."

"Thanks for the support! I'm just trying to keep things light; you two are like Gloomy Gus and his cousin, Despondent Dave. Anyway, I think I see the ocean."

You stare into the west. Looking at the gray blackness of early morning, you see a deeper movement in the sameness, and then the sun gives just enough illumination that you see the waves roiling in the vastness of the Pacific Ocean. It doesn't look peaceful now. As you get closer, flying over ever greener alpine meadows and windswept hill country, your eyes are captivated by the endless strength of the water hurtling itself at the land. The water was winning the fight.

"I guess the coast isn't that different here," Peter says as he moves the flyer towards the sea. "Because it is so mountainous near the coast, it just lost a little bit of ground. Not like Florida or the places that got hit by the tsunami."

"I think we're heading to that cove over there," Dresdale says, pointing. "At least, that's what the map says. Not much beyond here anyway."

Peter brings the flyer in for a smooth landing in a parking lot next to a massive pier that juts out into the froth of the sea. No one is around. There are no cars, and beside the parking lot and the road leading into the pier, there is almost no sign of humanity anywhere around you. It feels lost, desolate and alone.

"Man, it feels good to stretch!" Peter says, putting his arms out straight, letting the sunrise silhouette him. He drops his arms and turns toward the sound of a motor.

"Now what?" you ask, worried.

"I think your answer is coming towards us," Peter replies, pointing to the sea.

A medium-sized boat is racing toward the pier. Chop flies in the air as it bounces on swells and waves. The craft is low and black, and it looks like some sort of shark the way it disappears and reappears amongst the chaos of the ocean. Only at the last instant are the engines thrown into reverse with a loud squeal to avoid crashing into the immobile wood.

Two men throw open a hatch, hopping out onto the heaving deck. Moving with well-practiced ease, they secure the lines and jump onto the pier. They are wearing dark green foul-weather gear, with a glowing strip around each foot.

"What are you waiting for?" one of the men yells at you. "Get in the boat! Now!"

You stand there, not sure what to do. Part of you just wants to follow orders, to listen to the adult telling you what to do, but another part, equally strong, is wary of getting into a boat with total strangers who look rather menacing.

If you follow the man's orders and get in the boat, turn to page 62.

If you decide that you don't want to be rushed into a boat with strangers, turn to page 181.

Strange Chariots

W e don't have time to talk about it," the man continues. He has a full black beard and gold-capped teeth. You almost laugh, but you hold it in. "The Gatekeepers will be here any moment. Either come or be left behind. I'm not risking my freedom for you to wait like kids choosing ice cream flavors!"

You look at Peter and Dresdale. They are already moving to the flyer to grab your stuff. The two men help you with your limited supplies. You enter the boat as a wave crashes over it. Cold water in your face makes you gasp, but you continue on into the black ship.

"Man, look at all this gear!" Dresdale says as you move down a narrow gangway to the conn center. Screens, holo-projections, and camera views from above and below the water fill a small command center.

"Grab a seat," says a tall man dressed in a plain black jump-suit. He's in front of a control yoke that would look more appropriate on a starship than on a boat. "Use the six-point harness. We're going to be taking off at high speed."

"Thanks," you mumble, fumbling with the harness. "Um, who are you and where are we going?"

The man is flipping switches and cycling over a virtual keyboard, but he turns his head and stares at you. "This is so typical of this outfit! Did Jefferson meet with you? Did he tell you where to meet up with us? Did he tell you about the FFA? Hold on!"

The boat surges ahead. Acceleration grabs you and pulls you in like the embrace of a drowning man. A grunt comes out of your mouth and you see water and bright morning light as you smash through 20-foot waves. After a time, the force lessens and you get your bearings. Dresdale and Peter are giving high-fives in the back.

"Sort of," you answer, as if you had not been interrupted, as if you had not almost swallowed your tongue. "I met this man, I guess, who first pointed a shotgun at me and then told me to come here. He also told me about the Radiant Ones, but he didn't say who I would be meeting. And then he disappeared."

"I'm Lieutenant Ferris McMann, pleased to meet you. Man, that Jefferson is so crazy. We have so few friends, we can't always be choosy. Take a look at this bunch," he says, using his left hand to point at the other people crowding the small bridge. A couple of them chuckle, but no one looks up from their consoles. "Anyway, Jefferson is one of the two holo-projectors we have available to us. He's just a bit eccentric. I'm here to get you to the platform for the boss. She's in a huge hurry. We only found out about the Carlsbad situation two days ago."

"Do you know anything about my parents?"

"I'm sorry, but I haven't heard anything. Maybe the boss knows more, but she's not here."

"Okay, fine, but I have some other questions. How did you know where we were? What is a holo-projector? Where are we going?"

"And do you have anything to eat?" Peter adds, quickly noticing Dresdale's glare. "What? We basically ran out of food. I'm hungry!"

"Catch," Lieutenant McMann says, tossing Peter an energy bar. Peter snags it from the air, opens it and shares it with you and Dresdale. "Your parents' flyer has a tracking beacon that they installed for us when they got it. We knew where you were, but we didn't dare use ordinary means of contacting you. Things have been crazy the last few days. It's been a real shakeup. Gatekeepers have been swarming on us like a bunch of army ants."

"What's causing them to go after you now?" Dresdale asks, wincing as the boat slams down from the crest of a wave.

"I'd love to know," Lieutenant McMann says with a laugh. "We'll be there soon enough."

"For the third time: Where are we going?"

"We, meaning you, me, and your two friends, are only going a bit farther. Then you three will continue on, or down, rather, once we meet up with our, uh, other friends. You are in for a real treat; few have been so honored."

"I hope that your friends aren't as eccentric as the last one. I don't really like guns pointed at me."

"You don't have to worry about that! Our friends are a little strange though. Have you heard of the Elephant Whales?"

"I thought that was just something from trashy newspapers," Dresdale responds. "Aren't they supposed to be some sort of "super seal" or something? With trunks like elephants that they can use like hands?"

"Bingo, but they are closer to whales than seals. And smart. They use tools to hunt their prey, the giant squid. Smaller than the sperm whales, they have to spear their prey. At least the big ones."

"So, what do you mean when you say 'down'?" Peter asks. "And do you have any more energy bars? Preferably something without apricots?"

"Where did they come from?" you ask.

"They came from inside, and that is where they are going to take you," McMann says, and his words sound like the verdict from a judge. "They will take you inside to try and find your parents, before..."

"Before what?" Fear makes your voice rise.

"Before something bad happens."

Thoughts, images, and desire for a normal world bounce inside your head like stones in a polisher. Lieutenant McMann turns his attention to piloting and navigating his boat, ironically named No Name. "It used to be a smuggler's top boat before we got it and her title stuck." The rest of you pass the time in silence. Someone brings you some sandwich wraps, bottles of water and hot tea. You fall asleep once the rough seas ease.

"Put this on," one of the sailors on the boat says, handing you a drysuit. "The water's cold."

Before you know it, you are standing on the front deck of the No Name with Peter and Dresdale. The three of you are dressed in your drysuits and you feel a bit silly, not having

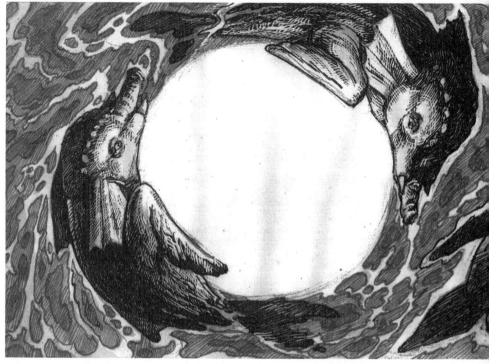

worn one before. Clouds have moved in and the sea is less rough. Not calm, just less rough.

"There they are!" McMann shouts into the wind.

Your stomach clenches in fear as you see a thick blue snake shoot out of the water. It is followed by a massive blue-black form, and an eye as big as a volleyball swivels around to stare at you. A jolt of intelligence seems to shine forth from the being from below. You feel as if you are in the presence of something ancient and wise, but also awesome with the meaning of awe closer to fear than adulation.

The snake-nosed whale opens its mouth and breathes out a fetid blast of air and water, reeking of ammonia and shellfish.

Large, serrated teeth form a rictus of a smile and the Elephant Whale emits a series of clicks, whistles, and squeals, similar to a dolphin, but deeper and more melodic.

"You might want to try a breath mint!" Peter offers helpfully, while looking nervous on the heaving deck of the boat.

Two other Elephant Whales emerge from the dark water, and they bring something to the surface with their trunks. Reaching and pulling, with their massive heads below the surface of the water, you see them lifting a sphere into the air. The sphere is opalescent and translucent, and even in the cloud-filtered light, it shines with the fluid rainbows of mother-of-pearl.

"Okay," says Lieutenant McMann. "Hop in. Your ride is here."

"What?" you splutter. "We're supposed to get in the water with those, uh, things? Look at their teeth!"

"Don't worry, dogs have teeth too, but if they're friendly it's no problem. These three are our friends; they won't hurt you."

"If you hadn't noticed," Peter adds, "these babies are a lot bigger than dogs! By like a factor of one hundred!"

"You two are the babies," Dresdale says, jumping into the dark water with the two Elephant Whales. Using strong, long strokes, she heads to the sphere in the rough chop. One of the Elephant Whales reaches up with its trunk and unscrews a hatch, opening the sphere for Dresdale. Another reaches its trunk from behind her.

"Watch out, Dres! One's coming for you!" Peter yells, but the trunk of the elephant-whale merely lifts Dresdale out of the sea and gently deposits her through the hatch and into the sphere.

Peter looks at you, and neither of you move or speak for at least a minute. Ever since you were a little kid, and you saw a scary movie about sharks, you have had a deep fear of the ocean. Actually, it wasn't the ocean so much, but a fear of the creatures in the ocean that could eat you.

"Feel like a dip?" Peter asks.

You nod. Peter takes your hand, which is sweating inside the confines of the drysuit glove, and you jump together into the sea. You doubt that you look as confident as Dresdale, but you manage not to scream when the trunk of one of the Elephant Whales lifts you into the sphere. Peter is right behind you, and the Elephant Whales secure the screw-on hatch with a bell-like clang. The whole sphere vibrates with the tone.

"Check this place out!" Peter says. Standing up and walking around the interior. "What do you think this stuff is?" he asks, pointing to the crystalline foam covering the floor, walls and ceiling of the sphere. The foam looks like transparent sponges growing on reefs of glass.

"Not sure," Dresdale replies. She has taken her hood off, and her hair surrounds her head in an auburn haze. "I think it is sort of like bubble-wrap or something. Most likely it is to keep us from getting hurt when this thing bounces around. It looks like there are some couches where we can strap in."

From outside the sphere you hear a loud trumpeting and squealing, and then you feel the whole sphere jerk with a movement counter to that of the waves.

"Hold on!"

Even though the sphere is translucent from the outside, you can see out of it with little distortion. Looking down, you see the three Elephant Whales pulling with their trunks on a long chain attached to the sphere. Each whale pushes with its tail and flippers, driving you down, down into the darkness of the sea.

"Man, look how strong those guys are!"

"Yeah, not only that, but they are supposed to be super-smart, too. McMann told me a bit more about them when we were getting ready. Do you two realize where we are going? We're heading into the Earth!! That's where these Elephant Whales are from. It's hollow in there!! This is so crazy!"

"Why don't the Elephant Whales colonize the outer world?" Peter asks. "Seems like they are pretty tough to me."

"Not sure, exactly, but McMann thought it might have something to do with lack of prey out here. Also, I guess the Inner Earth's ocean is a lot saltier than ours, so that may be another reason. Anyway, he said they had just formalized the alliance with the Elahw. That isn't their real name for themselves, and McMann laughed when he told me it."

"We really have no idea what we are getting into," you state dully. "It feels like some freaky amusement park ride, where you can't get off and it never ends."

"No way," Peter says with a grin. "This is much cooler than any amusement park ride. Take a look at those sea-gods pulling us all the way inside the Earth. It's like Apollo's chariot, only in the water, and with whales instead of horses!"

"More like Poseidon's chariot," Dresdale offers. "I'm going to get into something more comfortable than this drysuit and then I am going to enjoy the ride."

As you are pulled deeper into the ocean, the light from the surface fades. Soon you are in the deep indigo twilight of the depths. Still the Elephant Whales continue down, and all of the light from above soon disappears. However, once out of the disguising glare of daylight, you learn that your vessel is its own source of illumination. The whole sphere glows with a pinkish light that makes the Elephant Whales' skin look like congealed oil.

"We must be in some sort of trench," Dresdale observes after a long while. "It's hard to say how far down we are, but it seems like we are below where the ocean floor ought to be."

"Yeah," agrees Peter. "Shouldn't we be breathing some

helium or something? If we go down too far, won't we have to deal with decompression and the bends?"

"I don't know," you offer, "but I think if this sphere is pressurized we'll be okay."

"I guess we'll find out," Peter states, before adding in a strained falsetto, "but it would be more fun if we talked like overly-caffeinated mice!"

You watch in fascination as the Elephant Whales take a rest from their task and expel enormous bubbles of spent breath. Using their trunks they replenish their air by sucking air out of smaller spheres attached to the chain. Then they continue on, pulling you deeper and deeper.

You, Peter and Dresdale enjoy your first real meal since lunch of the day you were kicked out of school. The Elephant Whales had ferried over your gear while you were flailing about in the water, and Peter had managed to convey to Lieutenant McMann and the others just how truly hungry you all were.

"Man, that was good! Just what I needed," Peter says contentedly after polishing off a huge salami and turkey sandwich.

"I don't think I have ever seen anyone put a whole bag of potato chips in their sandwich before, though," Dresdale observes.

"Gives it a little crunch," Peter replies. "You should try it!"

Exhausted after all of the travel by flyer, boat, and bathysphere, the three of you fall asleep on the foam couches after your meal. Dreams of your parents being pulled by Elephant Whales to a massive black boat that turns into a shark make your sleep unrestful.

"I think we're in the Abyssopelagic or even the Hadopelagic zones," Dresdale says to you as you wake up.

"What does that mean?" Peter asks.

"It just refers to the levels of open water in the ocean. The Abyss and Hades parts come from Greek. You know, like the bottomless pit and the underworld."

"Sure, I know about that. Seems like it is sort of true, don't you think? I mean, we're going through a bottomless pit to the underworld, or at least the inner world," Peter says thoughtfully. "I wonder what it will be like."

"Different, for sure. Beyond that, I don't know," Dresdale replies.

The faint glow of the sphere illuminates only about twenty feet of the complete darkness of the deep. You are startled when you see rock walls surrounding the sphere. They are barren of any life, and you slide past them in silence.

Eventually you get the sensation that you are no longer falling, but rather that you are rising. Your spirits lift as you ascend. When you see light above you, you almost feel happy.

"Don't we have to worry about decompression syndrome or the bends or something?" Peter asks again, while performing some deep knee bends to illustrate his point.

"I don't know," you answer. "But I think we have to trust that they didn't send us in this thing just to make us sick."

"It all has to do with the pressure levels," Dresdale explains as she packs her gear into her backpack. "If the difference between pressures isn't that great, then no dissolved gasses will start re-gassing in your body. I never felt my ears pop, so I think we're probably at sea level pressure. Should we put our drysuits on?"

"I'm going to," Peter says. "I think I look pretty sweet in mine, even if it does have some dried salt lines."

The sphere is now floating ahead of the Elephant Whales, pulling them by the same chain that they pulled it with. The whales look listless, with only an occasional twitch of a flipper or fluke to indicate that they are conscious. While watching them you see them release the chain in a synchronized manner, and the sphere picks up speed without their drag.

"Strap-in!"

Breaking the surface of the inner sea with a loud splash, you float into the air for a moment, like a child's ball popping to the surface of a pool, and then crash down into the sea once again. You bob in silence for a few moments, and then see the Elephant Whales surface. They gulp greedily at the air, breathing through their mouths and trunks. After a few minutes, they grab hold of the chain and pull you towards a distant smudge of in the distance that looks like land. Soon it grows larger and you can make out the details of a rocky shore with a few small bushes and shrubs clinging to the higher portions of the terrain.

"What does it look like out there?" Peter asks as the Elephant Whales twist open the hatch of your strange chariot. You hold your breath, just in case the air is bad, but there is only a faint hiss of pressure equalization, so you stop holding it in and breathe deeply.

"Peter, stop shoving me, and I'll let you know," Dresdale answers as she peers out of the hatch.

The air is saltier-smelling than the Pacific, and it also has the scent of rotting seaweed or other vegetation. Dresdale moves out of the way, and you stick your head out of the hatch. You blink in pain from the red light streaming onto your face, and when you clear them, you see that there are people standing on the rocky shore nearby.

"Looks like we're about to meet our new friends," you say, moving so Peter can see. "Anyone else a bit nervous?"

"Not me," Peter responds. "It's showtime. Our whale buddies are bringing us in for a landing."

A tall woman wearing loose fitting white clothing throws a rope to Peter, who catches it smoothly and uses it to pull you in to the shore. Two men use long poles to keep the sphere from hitting the rocks. The woman reaches down with her hand and grabs Peter and pulls him onto the rock next to her. She is tall, with a long, straight nose and long black hair. Her skin is the red of gold in firelight, and her eyes are the black that comes when the fire is put out.

"Welcome," she says in accented English. Her voice is gentle, but full of spirit and strength. "I am Ama. We are honored to have you in the l and of the Forgotten People."

You steady yourself on the rocks after Ama has helped you on shore. The rocks, slippery from the seawater, are red, like almost everything else here. The two men with Ama push the sphere back into the sea once Dresdale and your gear has been offloaded.

"Thank you for the ride!" you yell to the Elephant Whales as they move the sphere out to sea once again. It shines with the red light of the tiny inner sun, and its opalescent surface shimmers with the wet spray. Two of the Elephant Whales pause and raise their trunks in the air as if in a salute and then give great blasts of trumpeting noise before sinking under the water and pulling the sphere behind them.

"They did you great honor by transporting you from the Old World," Ama says as you watch the spot where the sphere vanished mere moments before. You turn your attention to the woman talking to you and try to take in as much about your circumstances as possible. "It is a dangerous journey for them, and it has been forbidden until only very recently."

"They're beautiful, the Elephant Whales, I mean," Dresdale says to Ama and her companions. "Are they as smart as Lieutenant McMann said they were?"

"Our people believe that they are close to the gods, or even sometimes like the gods themselves. They traditionally keep to themselves, deep in the waters of the Sea of Tears. Only now, with the war against the Agarthans, have they begun to engage with us land-livers."

"Why is that?" Peter asks as you follow Ama up a steep path.

"I think it is because the Sea of Tears has changed so much. It is much higher and less salty than before. They are worried about this change, and they blame Sceptus and his Agarthans. Come, I will tell you more soon. There is much to learn and accept. It will be difficult, as we have no time and much to accomplish."

"I am sorry," you say, struggling to keep up with Ama, "but I don't even know who these 'Agarthans' are and what they have to do with my parents."

Ama stops and looks at you. Her face is surprised and fearful. "Hurry on, I will tell you all you need to know when we are safe from prying eyes."

You look around, expecting to see someone staring down at you, but all you see are rocks, the Sea of Tears behind you, and an occasional skittering lizard. Putting aside your desperate need for knowledge, truth, or even a crumb of sense from this crazy situation, you focus on following Ama and her friends. You try to heed Dresdale's advice and ride with the course of events.

Ama leads you to a cave, and you welcome the cool darkness, as you are hot and sweaty from the hike.

"Wow, this is a huge cave!" Peter says, trying to whistle, but managing only a dry hiss. "Look how smooth everything is! It's almost like glass or something."

"Yeah, it's definitely cool," you agree, pointing to some pueblo-style houses built against the curves of the cave's walls. "There's even a pool in the middle for water. This place looks really old."

"Welcome to Holeeloh. This is one of our oldest settlements," Ama explains as she leads you past the deep pool of water in the center of the cave. It is clear and fresh-looking, and you see a few pale white fish swimming lazily on the bottom, picking at the pebbles with their mouths. "And one of the few permanent places where the Forgotten live. Mostly we are nomadic, following the patterns of the inner sun. But there are always exceptions to who, or what, we are. Please come inside my domicile."

Ama holds open a curtain into one of the houses built into

the wall of the cave. Her silent companions must have left at some point, as they are no longer with you. The house's mud walls have been stuccoed with a pale brown plaster that leaves the surface shiny in the dimness of the cave. Ama's house is simple, with cushions and rugs on the floor and a simple cooking area with a small stove. A low table dominates the room, and maps are spread out all over it. Different colored crystals and rocks indicate specific places.

"Where are we?" Dresdale asks politely, gesturing vaguely at the maps.

Ama answers by pointing at a large white crystal in the center of the largest map. "This is Lighthome, the capital city of the Lemurians and Prince Torgan; we are here," she says indicating a point a good bit away, and marked by a small brown stone. "Over there is New Babel, citadel of the Agarthans, and the cause of our current woes." New Babel is marked by a thin, vertical crystal that pulses slowly in the dim light of the house. "That is where they have your parents!"

Your heart squeezes in surprise, and you lean forward to stare at the map. Now you know where your parents are! Relief wins its battle with worry for a quarter of a second before losing ground to the doubts and fears again.

"How can we get there?" you ask, trying to keep hope. "When can we leave?"

"We need to stock supplies for the journey. Right now our provisions are low. We are a hardy and strong people, but the war has strained our food stores to the point where we only have a few days left. We can spare very little. Our job is to help you as best we can, but we can't give you what you will need to go the whole way. Hopefully, a shipment from Lighthome will be able to make it here in the next week or so. You could go and meet the caravan and get supplies from them before traveling on to New Babel. It would be in the exact opposite direction, but you could help protect the food as it makes its way here. Once in our territory, you could leave the caravan and head off. We can spare three scouts and two soldiers to help you on your journey."

"Whoa, hold on there a sec, Ama," Peter says. "Is there another choice that you haven't told us about? Can't we find food on the way? It doesn't look that far away on this map."

"Maybe, maybe you could find food, but that map is deceiving. The journey is arduous, long, and risky, even when well supplied. To attempt it without proper food supplies would be foolish, and to do it in a time of war would be quite stupid."

"Why are you helping us?" you ask.

"You are the Child of the Child. The Elahw brought you through to this world. We need to help you find your parents for they, and you, are the keys to bringing down Sceptus and his empire. That is why, but we would help you anyway. The Elahw are not wrong; there is a goodness and a strength in you."

If you choose to meet the supply caravan, delaying your journey to find your parents in New Babel, turn to page 10.

If you decide to risk the journey to New Babel without proper supplies, turn to page 146.

Three Minus One Equals Zero

These, uh, people know where my parents are, and they can take me there. I have to go," you say to Peter and Dresdale.

Peter's face hardens, but he says nothing. Neila makes a sad little chirping sound. The cut on Dresdale's face has dried by now, but she looks like a crazed Amazonian warrior with the dirt, blood and exhaustion in her eyes.

"Are you coming with me?" you ask her, trying not to plead, hoping that she will say yes. Dresdale looks at Peter wistfully, then turns to you.

"I told you that I would help you find your parents," she answers, "and I meant that. I think we should go with Neila, as we would not be here without his help, but if you want to go to where your parents are, I will come with you."

"Thank you," you say, relieved.

Peter stalks away, but Neila peeks out of the backpack and gives a wave with his small, glowing hand. "Good luck!"

You go with the two Desera Fox People and your soul feels ripped apart as Peter heads in the opposite direction with the other s. Dresdale looks at you and you know that she is feeling the same way, as her face is twisted into a half-smile, half-snarl.

"I think I'm in shock," she says. "Why would Peter go with

Neila? I don't understand. We're his friends."

"I guess he found a new friend," you say bitterly. You think better and try to honor your friend with the right words, even if you don't feel the meaning they give. "Look, Dresdale, I wish Peter had come with us, but clearly he needed to go with Neila. It's like they formed some sort of bond back in the tunnels. I don't know, maybe what he is doing is important. Peter has been a great friend and I won't let this get in the way of that friendship. The fact that he came this far with me is an amazing, wondrous gift."

You follow the Desera Fox People back to their colony. It's an amazing cave complex carved out of the earth and stone of the alien landscape. Small sleeping chambers connect to middens, kitchens, meeting halls and storage areas. It's a troglodyte paradise.

"Do you think they could make the ceilings any lower?" Dresdale asks sarcastically as you crouch low to fit in the tunnels. Your guides flow through them like balls of fur sucked in by a vacuum cleaner, and you envy them their grace and suppleness. The Fox People are truly awesome. After your brief scuffle at the tunnel mouth, you know just how quick and agile they are.

After letting you use one of the sleeping chambers to rest and clean up ("No running water in here, I guess they just lick themselves clean!"), your guides bring you to a meeting with the colony's elders and generals. You learn this from a note written in English on a blackboard-like tablet. The hand-writing is very precise and small.

Child of the Child, please join us in the main chamber to develop plans to reclaim your parents, and to avenge the contamination done to the Lake of Dreams and the Hall of Warriors Gone. — Eldest Hunter

The meeting is mostly meaningless to you and Dresdale, as the foxes yip and bark and whine at each other. It is fascinating to watch these strange, intelligent, fox-people with their tools and accoutrements that seem almost human. You try to remember as many details as possible, but you know Dres will pick up more. At the end they hand you the tablet back with a new message.

The hunt has been set. The Agarthans who defiled the Lake of Dreams and the Hall of Warriors Gone are in a camp not far. If you and your friend wish to come, you may, Child of the Child. Your parents are in the camp.

— Hunter's Council

Before you know it, you and Dresdale are sitting in the back of a cart filled with supplies and pulled by a giant lizard that looks fully capable of eating you with one bite.

"Looks like they put us here to keep us safe and out of the way while they do the actual work," Dresdale says. The cart moves slowly over the rocky ground, and both of you are sore from the frequent bumps and lack of anything soft to sit on. You have been traveling throughout the dim-time of the inner world's night, and you guess that six or seven hours have passed when your life changes irrevocably in a bang and a flash. Your eyes burn from the brightness of the light.

"Oh my god!" Dresdale screams! "What happened?! Are you okay?! Oh my god...oh my god, your face!"

You keep blinking, but the afterimage does not go away. Then the pain from the blistering skin on your face hits you and you pass out, retching and writhing on the floor of the cart.

The booby-trap killed four of the Desera, and Dresdale suffered severe burns on her arms and back, but she recovers. You are never able to see again. The Desera take you to The Illuminated's outpost and Peter cares for you, Dresdale, and Neila until you all heal as much as you can. Most of the Agarthans were killed or captured by the Desera, but a few escape and they take your parents with them.

The End

Lighthome

As much as you want to play the hero, you know that you should go and get help before doing something stupid. It doesn't make it easier as you move away from the outcropping and the bats with their canisters filled with poison.

Durno's face flushes a deep yellow when you tell him about what happened. For the first time since you met him, he seems scared. Somehow that makes you like him a lot more, but at the same time, it increases your fear.

"Wake up everyone! We have to leave now!"

"What about the bats?" you ask, thinking that Durno would want to stop the poison attack on his people. "What about the poison?"

"What about being caught?" he fires back. "What about we get away and deliver a warning. 'Maybe we can catch them!' he mocks. Do you know who that is?"

Durno's fierceness is always there, but his intensity takes you back just the same.

"I am tired of caring for all you, you children," he splutters. "The man you saw is Bram, the heir to the Empire, along with his personal bodyguard, Morphus! If we can capture or kill either one it would be a great victory for us, but these are soldiers, warriors. You have no chance against them. To try would mean certain death. I would leave you to find out your foolishness for yourselves, but you would never get a chance to learn another lesson." He is exasperated. "I don't have time to explain everything now. Get moving!"

You don't argue with Durno. It's time to go. Dresdale and Peter look dazed, but continue to pack their few belongings and get ready to move out. Once you have gotten well away from Bram Interious, Morphus, and the bats with their deadly payload, Durno tells you: "This war we are in is a brutal struggle for survival. My heart burns to turn away now, but I know it would be useless. We are doing the only thing we can. I know people who drink that water—friends, relatives. I am scared for them."

Your sense of euphoria is gone, and you distract yourself from the pain of the hike by thinking about your consciousness swap with Bram Interious. What happened? Somehow you still feel a connection to him.

The sun gradually grows brighter and Durno gathers the six of you underneath a rock overhang. There is hardly room to breathe, let alone move, but Durno keeps all of you there for more than an hour. Keldso and Turina, other Lemurians, become still as rock. You, on the other hand, start bouncing your right leg absentmindedly. Dresdale pokes you in the ribs with her elbow.

"Cool it, dude, your bouncing is driving me nuts!" she whispers.

"Sorry," you reply. "I can't help it."

"Okay, now we can move," Durno says. You don't see how anything has changed, but he feels confident that somehow you are safer than you were.

For the third time in less than a day, you cross back over the ridgeline, continuing down into the valley. A few small houses with gardens and animal pens dot the landscape. There is no sign of anyone around.

"Maybe they saw the bats?" Dresdale murmurs when you point out the lack of people near the farms.

"What I want to know is, who was that Bram guy going to meet? It doesn't look like the power elite hangs out down here." you query.

"Who knows? With the road just up ahead, I'm sure that many people pass through here," Dresdale says, looking at the lonely homesteads before adding, "At least, near here!"

"Durno, tell us more about this Bram and his bodyguard. When I saw his face, I was knocked out by a green flash. I don't know if I was dreaming or what, but I was Bram for a little while. It didn't feel strange at the time, and I knew who I was and what I was doing. I was preparing to poison the water supply of a whole city!"

"How were you going to do it?" Dresdale asks softly.

"We were going to fly in on these giant bats and dump the poison in the reservoir," you say calmly, trying to remember. "Normally the water treatment facility would find the presence of so much poison, but we had bribed one of the technicians to rig the sensor so that it wouldn't go off."

"Whom did you bribe?" Durno asks, stopping and turning to look straight at you.

"I don't know," you reply. "We were going to meet them and give them their payment. Even though everything was different, it all felt normal. Like a dream, but much more real. It really happened. Everything that I saw was true. I don't think that makes sense, but you know what I mean. Anyway, it is all confusing."

"What hasn't been confusing?" Peter asks.

"That isn't helping any. You can help us by figuring out what this means!" Dresdale replies, rising to the bait. "This connection you have with this Bram guy is definitely weird, but it did help you get enough information to know to get out of there!"

"Does it have anything to do with the ritual the Lemurians put you though?" Peter asks. "There were plenty of green flashes during that thing."

"Yeah, I remember. It has something to do with it, but it was a different experience altogether than the Truth Enlightenment Ritual."

"Walk while you talk," Durno says, and you realize that he is saying it more to himself than to anyone else. "Bram and his bodyguard Morphus are the nightmare that makes our resistance to the Agarthan Empire so much harder."

"He's heir to the Emperor, right?" Peter says. "Then why would they send him on such a risky raid?"

"The Agarthans have a new society built on conquest. To that end, they have put in place an unofficial yet powerful requirement that their leader come from a background filled with bravery and danger," Durno answers, breaking into a trot as he urges you on. "He is young, but he has already done more as a warrior than most men ever will."

"Still, it seems bizarre that they would risk him like that,"

Peter pants. You suspect that Durno decided to run to keep Peter from interrupting him.

"He has Morphus to watch over him," Durno replies, as if that explained everything.

"Who is Morphus, then?" Peter gasps, struggling to speak while jogging.

"He is death," Durno says. "I saw him in person, just once, when I was younger. He led a group of cave walkers into the middle of a battle. He won, we lost. I lost my father to him. Come on! We need to get to the road." He picks up the pace and the conversation dies down.

Later, during a midday rest, when Durno, Keldso, and Turina are out searching for food, you can finally speak freely. "Now we know why Durno is so upset about this Morphus guy," you tell Peter and Dresdale. The three of you get up to clean the morning's dishes with sand and elbow grease.

"Work while you talk," Dresdale advises with a touch of vinegar.

"Morphus was responsible for his father's death!" Peter exclaims.

"Yeah, so you'd think Durno would do anything to destroy him, right?" you reply.

After a lunch of roots and water, you hit the trail again. At first, all of your attention is focused on the blisters on your feet, but you soon become inured to the pain, and you find yourself coming back to the bigger problems you have right now: where are your parents, where is Rimy, and where are you? Everything has been changing so rapidly in your life that it's hard to sort out all the thoughts and questions swirling in your head.

The valley with the scattered homesteads leads into a larger and broader valley. The road to the Lemurian capital of Lighthome lies against the first river you have seen since you have been in the inner world. Even after the mud storm, all of the arroyos are empty. In this wide valley a thin reddish stream keeps the road company as it winds its way down from the high plains above.

You see your first real plants since coming to this strange world. The trees and thickets that form a thin band along the riverbanks look normal, but instead of green leaves, everything is red. The trunks are brownish, but they also have a slight red tint. One tall tree looks like a weeping willow, but the scarlet leaves on the long whitish whips make the it look like blood dripping off of bones.

"Common chlorophyll adaptation," Dresdale mutters. "This sun must be emitting a broader spectrum than just the red band."

You ignore her and look at the road. It's deserted. Even though you are not an engineering student, you appreciate the scale of the project before you. Smooth, flat, and made of a dark red material, the road looks new, except for shallow wear marks in two parallel tracks.

"Is this road new, Durno?"

"New? Far from it; this road was here before we Lemurians came to the inner world millions of years ago. It's always been here, and it will be here always. It is one of the gifts from Magantha-God of Rock."

"What is it made of?" you ask, staring at the smooth rock below. Despite its smoothness, your tread is secure as you trot along.

"No one really knows. The closest match would be a type of crystal," Durno replies. "Hold on! Someone is on the road behind us. Put on your visors, and say nothing! We can't risk having you taken. Even if they appear friendly, do not reveal yourselves."

You slip the helmet visors down, covering your faces.

No dust rises behind you to announce the presence of anyone following. Once again you are amazed by Durno's awareness of the world around him. You look at the road, and notice that there is no dirt anywhere on its surface. Only inches away from the road, you see a thick layer of grime and dust almost covering a small boulder. Something keeps the road clean. But what?

Glancing nervously over your shoulder, you are rewarded with a small speck of movement in the distance. Two tan animals pulling a covered wagon slowly overtake your group. Durno pulls you over to the side of the road to wait for the wagon. Durno's right hand is inside his cloak, and you suspect that it is on the handle of his obsidian knife.

When the wagon draws near, Durno yells out a greeting and then begins to chatter with the wagon's driver. You can't catch a word, so you study the driver and his vehicle. The two beasts in front look like flattened camels. They snort and paw at the road when the driver stops. One gives you a mean look, and you decide not to go close.

You think that the driver is a Lemurian, but it is hard to tell underneath a wide-brimmed hat and dirty scarves. Thick leather gloves cover the hands of the driver, and you notice a knife handle sticking out of a belt. The wagon's only impressive feature is that the four wheels look like they are made out of blown glass. Thin, wispy and clear, you are amazed that they can support the weight of the wagon.

Dresdale nudges you in the ribs and whispers, "Durno got us a ride!"

"How do you know?" you whisper back.

Dresdale looks at you like you are stupid. "I have been paying attention. Maybe you should try it sometime."

Peter laughs and Durno stares at him and then he starts laughing, too. Even though he is not actually human, Durno is becoming more of a person to you. You think that he is just as stressed by all the responsibility on his back as you are.

Durno, Keldso, and the driver sit outside on the wagon seat, while you, Turina, Peter, and Dresdale climb into the wagon. It is cramped with the four of you inside. You stretch out on one of the bunks, trying to get some sleep. At the top of the peaked roof is a small cage holding a red lizard. The lizard flits about its cage singing trilling songs like a bird. Peter tries to get it onto his finger, but the small creature cowers in the back of its cage.

"Wake up, sleepyhead," Dresdale commands as she nudges your shoulder. You sit up quickly and almost bang your head. Sometimes you learn from your mistakes. Only sometimes, though.

"Come on, you're worse than a lazy eighth grader! Durno says we are about to get to Lighthome! Don't you want to see it?"

"Did I look asleep? Are we actually there yet? Can you answer me those two questions?"

"You are such a grouch sometimes," Dresdale says with a smile. "I don't even know why I came on this crazy trip with you."

"Because my parents were kidnapped and I asked you to," you reply. Her smile disappears.

"Yeah, that's right. I must have forgotten. Anyway, I'm going to peek through the curtain and see the Lemurian capital."

Peter and Turina are laughing in the other corner of the wagon. Peter taught her how to play rock-paper-scissors and they both laugh hysterically whenever they throw rock at the same time. You don't get it, so you close your eyes again. You know you should take Dresdale's offer and at least look at the city that the Lemurians call their capital. The more you know about your surroundings, the better off you'll be, but you just can't bear to do it. All you want to do is be home with your mom and dad. The loneliness stabs at your belly and you take in a deep breath of air.

"You okay?" Peter asks, still laughing with Turina.

"I'm fine," you say, sounding stronger than you feel.

You drift into a half-asleep, half-awake state where you know you have something you need to do, but you can't remember what it is. Somehow you also know that you are running out of time. You become fully awake when the wagon comes to an abrupt stop.

"Time to get out and see the city," Dresdale announces brightly. She opens the door and hops out. Peter and Turina follow her. You are the last one out.

You are in an ordinary looking grey stone courtyard. Except for the Lemurians, the strange draft animals with forked tongues, and the red sun that burns like an angry sore in the sky, you could be back home. You realize you are grasping at anything to contain your feeling of alienation. Nothing really looks like home. Even your friends seem to look different than before.

You step down from the wagon. Two sets of hands reach up to help you. Lemurians dressed in uniforms scurry about; they seem to be on urgent missions. Durno pays the driver in silver; you see the flash of the coins as he hands them over.

"What are those animals called?" Dresdale asks, pointing.

"They are the lifeblood of our world," Durno explains. "They are called surros, but that would translate to something like 'rock camels' in your language. I spent a lot of time tending the surros when I was little. They are usually friendly, but they will bite if scared," he says rolling up his sleeve to show a pale arm with a jagged scar along his forearm. "Right now we need to go meet Prince Torgan, we have much to share."

"Durno wants you to tell the commanders about your encounter with Bram Interious and his bodyguard," Dresdale informs you as Durno waves you forward.

The driver waves goodbye happily, taking his wagon outside the gate and into the city. You glimpse a crowded street outside the courtyard. The gate closes.

Durno leads the way into a large fortress-like building.

Finding a bored-looking soldier, he taps him lightly on the shoulder. It's clear that the soldier recognizes Durno, his eyes widening and his pale face turning slightly yellow. Saluting crisply, he speaks with Durno and then scurries off through a door.

"We'll be seen shortly," Durno says. He looks weary and begins to massage his temples. "Unfortunately there is no time for us to clean up before the meeting. Our information is too important to delay."

"Hey, no problem," Peter says. "I can probably go a couple more weeks without a bath, as I am naturally clean-smelling. Now Dresdale on the other hand, she'll probably need two baths."

"Very funny, ha-ha," Dresdale replies, pretending not to care about Peter's teasing. Later, you see her sniffing at her shirt. You know that you are smelly, but you don't really care.

Two Lemurian soldiers lead your group up a long, winding staircase that climbs into a stone tower. Narrow vertical windows break the walls of the tower staircase, but there's no time to look out and see where you are. You are comforted that the stone is not red, but rather a soft bluish-grey. It is soothing to your tired eyes. Lighthome is starting to grow on you. You come to the top of the tower where a small Lemurian male sits at a desk in front of a tall shuttered window.

Your guides speak with the little man. He then rises up onto his tiptoes, and throws the top latch to the shutters. Reaching down, he unfastens the other latch and opens the shutters. The baleful red eye of the micro-sun looks in the window, but your attention is focused on the city spread out in front of you.

Pink sand-drip-style buildings crowd your near view, looking like half-melted triple strawberry ice-cream cones, while over to the right, boxy black buildings with no obvious windows or doors tower into the sky. Scores of flying lizards with trailing leather pouches fly through the air. Some are bright red, while others are brown, dun, or yellow. You can't count them, they are so many. They look bigger than any bird you have seen in your life.

"Holy smokes, this is crazy!" Peter says, stepping towards the window.

"Amazing," Dresdale agrees, "but you both missed a lot when we first came into Lighthome. Peter was too busy flirting with Turina and you were too busy feeling sorry for yourself."

Peter looks at you as if to say, 'What did I do?' You play dumb and look at the windowsill. That is when you notice that the windowsill has a translucent wire bridge leading to another tower that is part of a small castle, about 200 yards away. The wire looks like a zipline, but with four strands instead of one. The first soldier steps up smoothly onto the bridge and steps out into the air. He turns back and motions to you.

"Don't worry, we have safety clips," Durno says, stepping forward onto the bridge. You notice that he does not take one of the safety straps held by the little man.

Dresdale steps forward, takes one of the straps, waits while the little man attaches it, and walks out onto the bridge. "A bit breezy," she says jauntily, but her grip is tight.

You wait until it is just you and the last soldier left to cross. He motions to you to get on the bridge. Forcing yourself to smile, you move forward and take one of the clips. The wires feel too thin to hold you, and they are cold to the touch. You tell yourself not to look down, and you do a good job with that until you are just about to step onto the bridge. You are directly above a river filled with a jumble of sharp rocks. The tower you are moving toward sits on an island set in the middle of the river. You finally notice what has been making the subliminal roar that you have been feeling in your bones, but only now know as a sound with your ears.

Someone taps you on the shoulder. It's the soldier. Smiling, he points forward forcefully. You cross the bridge only because you know you have no other option. If you want to find your parents, you have to keep moving forward. Fear must be overcome.

On the other side of the bridge stand two huge Lemurian soldiers. They politely search each of you, including Durno, Keldso, Turina, and the two soldiers who are your escorts. Durno looked longingly at his knife when they took it from him, but he did not protest.

"On to the big show!"

"We will be meeting with Crown Prince Torgan and his advisors," Durno tells you as you leave the top of the second tower. "Try to remember as much as you can about your experience—even something tiny may be the key to beating the Agarthans."

"I'll try," you say. Anxiety washes over you.

You are searched again at the door to the prince's meeting chamber. Somehow you get the sense that they are only careful because they have to be. That makes you feel even worse than before.

As you enter Prince Trogan's meeting room, you are surprised to see that everything is wooden. The room is small and circular, with built-in benches and tables. It has the feel of a courtroom. One seat is raised and larger than the others. You assume that the pale white Lemurian sitting there is the Crown Prince. He looks bored.

"Omigosh! Look who's here!" Dresdale exclaims, clutching your arm and pointing across the room. Sitting next to the prince is Sublimas-Chaeko. He notices Dresdale pointing and nods at you solemnly.

"How did he get out of the council room? I thought that he and Rimy were captured there."

"I don't know, Dres," you answer. "Let's see what happens."

Prince Torgan rises and makes a short speech in Lemurian. Dresdale nods her head, but you still fail to understand anything. Torgan moves forward and pulls a thin blue crystal out of a bone-colored scabbard. He places it in a stand sitting on the table nearest him. The crystal glows with a blue light, lifts up from the stand and hovers in mid-air. Torgan speaks again, and you hear an English translation coming out of the crystal.

"There, I think I got it working...yes, yes, I put it in heads up," the voice from the crystal says. "Welcome! I am Crown Prince Torgan, and I want to be the first to welcome you, Child of the Child, to our humble city of Lighthome! I am embarrassed to ask, but we need your help. You are the Emerald Warrior."

Prince Torgan bows towards you as he finishes speaking, and the crystal completes its translation seconds later, like a

poorly dubbed movie where the lips are out of synch with the voices. All of the others sitting on the far side bow their heads toward you, including Durno, Turina, and Keldso. You're thinking they must have you confused with somebody else.

"Uh, thanks, I guess," you mumble quietly. The crystal picks up your words and translates them into Lemurian. "What do you mean by the Emerald Warrior? I am not any kind of warrior; there must be some mistake."

"They didn't tell you?" Prince Torgan asks, surprise written plainly on his pale face. He is beautiful in a cold way. "You are the one we've been waiting for! According to the seers, your arrival has been whispered by the drips in the deepest limestone caves, by the ruffling of the night bats' wings, and by the shifting of the red dust dunes. You are our connection to Orana! Look, you have to help us, we're desperate. We can hold out for a while, but Sceptus and his legions grow stronger each day, while we grow weaker. Any loss for us is almost irreplaceable. Children are a rare and treasured gift, we have so few...anyway, I'm tired and bored of meetings that numb the mind, but you are important! We need your help."

Seeing your confusion, Torgan continues a bit less forcefully. "Please, I can see that you have been through much, and you are weary from the road, but Durno sent word that he had important news to give us. Please tell us about your encounter with Bram Interious."

Even though your encounter with Bram was brief, it takes time to explain what happened. Torgan asks many questions, and has you repeat things so that he knows exactly what happened. As you finish, you make one final plea to the crown prince.

"Your Highness," you begin, hoping that you are using the right term; you aren't used to talking to princes. "I will try and help you, but I just want to find my parents, and Rimy, too. If there is anything you can do, I would truly appreciate it."

"You have helped us simply by being the Emerald Warrior," Torgan replies. "You are helping us. With the information you have given us, we can see into the mind of the enemy. Our Thought Weavers will have much cloth to work with tonight! Anyway, we have a favor we need to ask of you first. This is what we need you for, Child of the Child, Emerald Warrior."

"Here it comes," Peter warns. "Watch out, and don't say yes until we have time to think about it."

"We need you to help us find Orana," Torgan says, via the voice from the blue crystal. "We have suffered mightily during the war with the Agarthans. With our current allies we have a chance of holding out against the Agarthans, but eventually they will break through. All of us will be brought under their rule, excepting those of us who are killed outright. We have been called vampires, falsely. That is how Sceptus began his quest for domination, by spreading lies and slander. We are to be killed to the last, so you can always count on our utmost dedication in the fight against Sceptus," Torgan pauses for a long moment before continuing. "We are arranging an expedition to the Great Cave, and we need you to help us find the entrance to Orana. Since the Ritual of Truth Enlightenment, you have carried a piece of Orana in you, and that piece will lead you to its home."

Torgan pauses, licks his pale lips, and continues on. "However, there are other considerations for you to know about. The trip will be dangerous. The Great Cave is in territory controlled by the Agarthans. Getting to the cave entrance itself will take much hard work, and maybe a lot of luck as well. You are our guest. You are not a Lemurian, and we cannot make you go on this trip for us. All we can do is make this most humble request."

"There is one other piece of information, though, and I am sure my advisors would have me keep this from you," Torgan says, glancing at Sublimas-Chaeko. "But we received a message from one of our spies in the Agarthan capital city of New Babel. They are holding two prisoners there, a man and a woman. Rumor is that they are 'magicians' from the world outside the world."

"My parents?" you ask, interrupting Torgan. "Do they have my parents there?"

"We do not know. Our spy is not someone whom we trust completely and his information was incomplete. That is all we have. I tell you of this because I want you to know that we are not holding anything back from you. I ask you again, will you help us find Orana? If you will not, we will still give you aid if you want to go to New Babel and look for them. I would not recommend that you do so. Emperor Sceptus takes a lion as his symbol, and you would be going into his den."

"Trap," Durno says flatly. "Don't fall for it."

"What is Orana?" you ask. "And why am I so important to finding it?"

"You hold a piece of Orana in you, and that will help you

find where that consciousness resides—we hope," Torgan replies. Sublimas-Chaeko seems uncomfortable with what Torgan is telling you, but the Prince continues. "Orana was the first here, in the Hollow Earth. All others came after. No one in memory has been with the physical reality of Orana, but many have been touched by its presence. You have been so touched."

"I need to think," you say. "I am so tired that my brain is bouncing right now."

"You may go now, but we will need your answer by the morning," Torgan says, picking up the crystal.

"What do you think?" you ask Peter and Dresdale. You are in a small, private room with food, water, and no windows.

"I don't like either choice," Peter offers. "One sounds like a religious mission, and the other sounds like it could be a trap like Durno warned."

"I think we should go for the Orana expedition," Dresdale says. "It sounds like it will actually help in this war! Besides, I had never met a god before, 'Child of the Child,' or is it 'Emerald Warrior'?" She winks at you good-naturedly.

"I never asked to join a war," you say wearily. "I just want to get my parents back."

If you decide to help Prince Torgan with his expedition to find Orana in the Great Cave, turn to page 132.

If you want to investigate the rumors that your parents are being held prisoner in New Babel, turn to page 41.

Continued from page 27.

Light in the Darkness

Dresdale gives you a worried look. You sense that something is disturbing Peter. You have all been stressed by the craziness of the last few days, but you can't help but wonder what effect Neila's presence has had on him. You hope that you are just worrying over nothing, but it's hard to dismiss your doubts and fears in the dusty darkness of the stone stairwell. Eventually even these thoughts fade again as you fall into the monotony of putting one foot in front of another.

"We're almost here!" Peter whispers after you come to a landing. "The opening is just around this corner."

Turning your head, you see drawings and writing etched into the rock walls along the landing. You see small glowing figures and tall, burning shapes: The Illuminated and t he Radiant Ones. You don't recognize any of the other strange figures in the drawings. Dresdale puts her hands out to touch the drawings, and you can see her brain trying to decipher the code of the writing. Peter beckons you with waves of his hand.

At the end of the landing, a huge rock blocks the way, but Peter merely slides by it and you follow. You are now in a small cave. Reddish light falls into it from the entrance. The light hurts your eyes and you squint as you make your way to the exit.

"Wow! Look at this place!" Dresdale says as she leaves the cave. "I've never seen anything like this."

You follow her and Peter, eager to get out from underground. Looking out into this strange new world, your brain struggles to understand what it is seeing. Directly above you is a tiny sun, burning with a fierce red light, while thin, dirty looking clouds scud across the sky. Red boulders are strewn about like the blocks left behind by giant children, and the horizon line is exactly opposite of what you are used to. You are still trying to figure that out, when you feel a sharp pain in your back and you pitch face first into the red dirt.

"Hey! What are you doing?!" Peter yells. "Let go!!"

Hands grab you and pull you upright. Luckily no dirt got in your eyes, but you accidentally swallow some and do your best to spit it out while you take everything else in. The creature standing before you is not a human being. It has a long, fur-covered snout, and its snarl reveals a mouthful of sharp teeth. It holds a spear threateningly in front of your face. Loud, high-pitched yelps and whines come from its mouth, and you sense that it is trying to ask you something, but of course you have no idea what it wants. You would raise your arms in submission, but they are held tightly behind you by one of the creature's friends.

Neila's sing-song voice rings out in the dusty air, but you can't tell what he is saying. The creature in front of you stops snarling and looks at you quizzically, but it does not lower the spear.

"Yeah, that's right, Neila! Tell them we mean no harm!" Peter says urgently. He and Dresdale are being held by more of the wolf-like creatures. Dresdale has a cut on her cheek; the thin line of blood looks black in the reddish light.

Neila keeps singing, and gradually you see the creatures relax. Eventually the one holding you lets go and jumps back. You shake out your arms, and before you even see it move, you feel the blunt end of the spear smacking you in the chest. You hit the ground hard on your butt. It hurts and you glower at your attacker.

"These are the Desera Fox people!" Neila yells out in English. He is half in, half out of Peter's backpack. One foot is caught in the straps, and you notice that he is missing his Pooh-bear sneaker on that small, glowing foot. "Don't resist! Hurt you bad if enemy!"

Neila switches back to his sing-song again, and the Desera Fox people sit down and listen to his story. They bark and whine back, but Neila seems to understand them, and they understand him.

"Is very good, Child of the Child," Neila says to you. "Glad I am that they did not hurt us, or us them."

"Not much chance of us hurting them," you say, rubbing your sore butt. "They had us wrapped up before I saw a thing."

"Listen what I say," Neila implores. You can tell that he is tired and frustrated. "We lucky here. Desera Fox know about Child of Child's parents! Came through Desera Fox Cave of the Dead. Very holy place. Agarthans came too. Met them. Took them away. Killed many. Disturbed spirits. These here go after to revenge living and dead. Hunt them down. One take me, Neila, to home. Get medicine. Get help. You go with them. You go with me. Choose."

"Huh," Peter says. "What are you saying, Neila? These dog-people will take you to your home? I'll go with you."

"Peter! Didn't you hear what Neila said? They located Mr.

and Mrs. Torman! They're going after them! Don't you think that is what we should do? That's what we came for!"

"Of course I heard him! Don't you think I don't know what he said? He needs our help though, now, and these guys won't be able to do it. You two can go on the revenge raid, but it sounds like a suicide mission to me. I'm going to help Neila. Once he is home and safe, we can go after the Tormans!"

You are too shocked to say anything at the moment.

"They go now. We go now too," Neila says.

If you decide to go on the revenge raid in the hopes of finding your parents, turn to page 79.

If you decide to help Neila get home first, turn to page 107.

Friends and a Hard Place

You are stunned that you have to make such a hard choice, but you don't voice your internal conflict.

"Fine," you say with more than a tinge of sarcasm, "if you think getting Neila home is more important than helping me find my parents, then that is what we will do. I don't want to leave you here to fend for yourselves."

Dresdale gives you a sad sort of look. You feel bad about trying to lay a guilt trip on Peter, but, still, you spoke your mind. You can't let him go off by himself in this strange inner world without your help. As you fret about having created hard feelings between you, you realize that Peter does not appear to have registered what you said as he focuses on Neila, who seems about to slip back into unconsciousness. Before he fades, Neila speaks some more with the Desera Fox people, and most of them head into the cave mouth. Two of them stay with you, joining Peter in hovering over Neila. They chirp and whine; the growls are gone.

"Where are their friends going?" Dresdale asks you, but Neila answers. His voice is weak but still beautiful.

"They go to dip in the water. Make holy the weapons of war. Make deadly. Make true."

"I guess it is some sort of purification ritual or something," Dresdale muses. "A lot of primitive cultures have superstitions about places with holy water and stuff."

"Not primitive!" Neila says with an edge to his song-like voice, rising from his prone position. "Desera know the secret of the Lake of Dreams. Sceptus not like it when he find out!"

With that, Neila subsides and Peter sends a cold stare in Dresdale's direction.

"We need to get Neila to his people," Peter says with a note of command tinged with panic. "He doesn't need you two stirring him up! Besides, these Desera folks know this place a lot better than we do. I'd be careful before jumping to any conclusions."

"What'd I do?" Dresdale whispers into your ear. "Why is Peter acting so strangely?"

You just shrug, not knowing the answer to the question.

Meanwhile, Peter and the two Desera have rigged Neila into the backpack with a platform supporting his head. They stand up, gesturing for the three of you to follow. You take time to override your conscious thinking. You look out upon the strangeness of the landscape that confronts you. You are alert.

Eyes having grown accustomed to the dim, red light, you try to understand how the Earth can be tilting upwards, as if you are in the bottom of some enormous mixing bowl filled with red lumps of earth-sugar and dirt-flour.

Having spent time in New Mexico, you are used to the stark palette of the desert, but this is completely different. The reds and blacks and tans are strange and unfamiliar. None of the shapes make sense in your brain. You realize that you are reacting on an instinctual level, not a thinking one.

Peter grabs you, snapping you out of your reverie.

"Get your act together!" he says. It is so unlike him that you wonder what has happened. "We need to move out."

"Hey, I'm not a marine in some stupid war movie!" you shout into his face. "I'm just trying to get my bearings. Everything about this place seems wrong, twisted, and alien. Give me a damn moment!"

"I'm sorry," Peter says, with deep weariness in his voice. "I just don't know what to do. Neila is dying! I can feel it. If he doesn't get home soon it will be too late."

"Why do you care? We just met him. What can he mean to you?"

"I can't explain, but I know that I do. He is light itself. He is good. He needs me as much as he needs anybody, if not more. He needs my help, and I have to give it. You don't understand. Neither of you do."

"Listen, Peter," Dresdale says as she puts a hand on his shoulder. "We're trying to help. We are trying to understand. This hasn't been easy for any of us. Just a few days ago my biggest worry was that I had a crush on Jake Garrity and he didn't seem to know that I even existed. Now I don't know where I am or what we are doing. But what I do know is that people have been chasing us, trying to kill us, trying to do who-knows-what to us!"

"You have a crush on Jake Garrity?" you blurt, with shock and disgust fighting for first place.

"Yeah," Peter says, chiming in without pause, the uncon-scious Neila on his back forgotten in the moment of shared outrage. "He is such a jerk!"

"A meathead!" you add with derision and condemnation. "How could you like someone like that? Do you remember how he stuffed Peter into a locker in 3rd Form?"

"Thanks for bringing that up," Peter says sarcastically. "But seriously, he isn't really that smart. He may have even fallen out of the stupid tree and hit every branch on the way down. I can't believe you didn't even tell us. I thought we were your best friends!"

Dresdale gives both of you a withering look. "I had a feeling you'd react like this, and I see that I was right. Anyhow, my point was that it was merely a crush. I was able to discern that at the time, but it would have been nice to have confided in my best friends without being greeted with scorn and mockery. I think Neila needs us to start moving, no?"

With that Dresdale turns around and marches off toward the two Desera Foxes standing in the dim red light.

"Wait!" you shout. "I'm sorry! I didn't mean it the way it sounded!"

Dresdale ignores you and turns her attention to the foxes. She motions for them to lead, and they do. Although smaller than you, they show great strength and agility clambering over boulders. Their large, furry ears swivel ceaselessly. What are they listening to, you wonder. All you hear is the sound of a dusty wind.

The Desera Foxes move quickly. They have to wait up frequently. During one of these breaks, while you and Dresdale wait for Peter to catch up, she shares her canteen of water with you. The water is surprisingly cool and sweet, and you feel an electric thrill as it fills you with its wetness

"Wait! This is the water from the Lake of Dreams, isn't it?"

"I think so, but I'm not sure. Neila said it was fine to drink."

"He also said that the Desera were going there to get blessed or something." What if it gives you strange dreams?"

"I wouldn't worry about it," she says, but you do.

The tiny speck of a sun becomes dimmer than before, but does not seem to move. Your furry friends call a halt and erect a fairly large tent made out of a red cloth that they unwrap from their midsections. Using their paw-like hands, they take the soft cloth and stroke it. Where they stroke it, the cloth becomes rigid. Soon they have created a shape like a turban, but without the head. They carefully reshape the contours of the structure until it looks like one of the thousands of other boulders you have passed since you started your hike.

"This is pretty cool stuff," Peter says with admiration as he inspects the camouflaged rock-tent. "I wonder how they do it."

"Must be some sort of on-off switch when they rub it," you offer, hoping that makes sense.

Meanwhile, the foxes have set up a small camp stove with a purple flame. They roast pieces of meat on the end of thin, sharp-looking knives. They offer you some, bowing slightly.

"Uh, thanks," you say, gingerly taking the steaming chunk of meat off the knife. "What is it?"

The foxes give little yips, and once again you wish you understood their language. You are surprised when Neila pipes up.

"Is lizard. Big lizard. Dragon lizard. Makes you strong, like dragon lizard," he says. He puts his small, glowing hands above his head to indicate how large the lizard is.

You take a small bite and are pleased by the smoothness and lack of gaminess in the meat. "It's good," you mumble. "Thank you."

"Neila, can you tell them 'thanks, but no thanks' from me? In as polite a way as possible?" Dresdale asks before turning to you and chuckling. "Aren't you supposed to say 'tastes like chicken'?"

"I would," you respond. "But it doesn't really. It has a more earthy taste. Smoky, but in a bland way. If that makes any sense."

"Not really," she says, ripping open an energy bar and washing it down with more water from the Lake of Dreams.

After your dinner you all huddle inside the tent, trying to get comfortable so you can. Unfortunately, it's practically impossible on the hard rock. At least the tent warms up from body heat. You worry about being depleted from lack of sleep, but you are so tired that you fall asleep while thinking that you'll never fall asleep.

You dream of your parents. You are at home, and they keep going off to their office. You go to look for them, but they are never in the office when you get there.

"Rise and shine, sleepyhead," Peter says mock-gently as he shakes your shoulder. "Yip and Yap want to get going."

"Yip and what?"

"You know, the foxes. I got tired of just calling them that. Neila said that there is no real translation to their names, so Yip and Yap were the closest I could come."

You scoot out of the low door of the rock-tent and watch

as Yap strokes the outside of the tent. It collapses like a parachute to the ground, and the two foxes deftly wrap the material around themselves. They throw you small dried fruits kind of like dates.

"How far away are we from Neila's friends?" you ask Peter as you hike across shifting red sand. A string of concave mountains blocks your view ahead.

"He said it won't be too far. There is a small community of The Illuminated in the mountains ahead. They should be able to help him. I hope. I could barely wake him up this morning. He seems worse."

You don't say anything, concentrating on the climb. As you get into the foothills of the mountains, you struggle more and more as the trail gets steeper. Jagged fallen rocks block your path. Twice Yip and Yap have to lower ropes to help you over larger obstacles. Finally they point to a higher mountain and gesture excitedly. You make out a smudge of green in the distance. It looks like mold clinging to the side of bread.

You are exhausted by the time you reach the smudge of green, but the amazing difference of this place energizes you. Small green trees with thick, frond-like branches sprout from the most unlikely places, such as cracks in the rock.

"Kind of like an aloe-plant fern or something." Dresdale muses. "But look how large some of these babies are!"

You follow a path to a pool of water bubbling out of the ground. This must be the source that feeds the greenery. Near the pool, a dark cave entrance yawns like the jaws of a whale. You are not eager to go back underground, but Peter plows straight ahead toward the entrance. Yip and Yap stop to drink from the pool and fill their bottles, and Dresdale does the same. You follow Peter into the cave.

At first you think the cave dead-ends, but after staring straight ahead for awhile, you see a shimmer of movement in the darkness. Peter heads towards the blackness and disappears.

"Peter! Wait up!" you shout. The blackness gives you a static tingle as you pass through it. Ahead of you is light. Glowing so brightly that you have to shield your now-tender eyes, you see five of the Illuminated surrounding a large crystal that juts up from the cave floor. The crystal glows with veins of bluish light. It pulses with an odd, five-part rhythm. As soon as the small, glowing people see you, they break away from the crystal, and the light from it dies immediately.

"He needs help!" Peter shouts. "He's really sick!"

The Illuminated gather around Peter as he kneels down. Gently, they remove Neila from the backpack and carry him deeper into the cave. Two stay behind, and they sing to you with voices of light and crystal liquid. It is one of the most beautiful things you have ever heard, but you don't understand the significance.

One of the Illuminated scurries away and then comes running back holding a small, glowing crystal. It sings again, and you hear an English translation coming out of the vibrating crystal.

"Thanks to you, who brought home our wanderer. We have been told of the tragedy. We have been told how the Radiant Ones came upon you. You are to be honored."

"Is he going to be all right?" Peter asks anxiously. You notice that Dresdale and the Desera have now joined you beyond the veil of darkness.

"It is hoped," replies the Illuminated via the crystal. Peter does not look reassured. "Come with us, we will give you our thanks. We will share our food. You have been through much."

They lead you out of the darkness and into the light. Leaving the cave, you feel a freedom from the earth, and you are glad to be beneath the strange sun and sky. One of the Illuminated takes your hand and guides you along a path beyond the pool and its coolness. You and your friends follow them mutely, acceptingly, and you notice that the Desera break away from your group and head down a different path. The trail steepens and you are amazed by the agility and strength of the Illuminated as it clambers over the rocks and roots. Neila had never displayed such vigor in the short time you had been with him, and the glow coming from this Illuminated was stronger and steadier than that cast by Peter's charge.

"We are almost there," says the crystal in your hand. You somehow hadn't noticed when the Illuminated gave it to you to carry earlier, when you had gotten to a steep incline. You nearly drop it in surprise. "You will need rest and food. We will gladly give you both."

"Thanks," you respond dully. You are so overwhelmed that you can't think or feel or talk properly. Too much information is battling for prominence in your mind. However, exhaustion is swiftly starting to win the battle over anything else. You follow the Illuminated into a small wooden pod clinging to the edge of a cliff like a grape glued to a rock. Inside are four small moss-covered beds.

"Drink this," the crystal orders. This time you don't jump. The Illuminated hands you a small gourd. You drink from it. It is sweet and nourishing and cool. Stumbling with fatigue, you shuffle to one of the small beds, lie down, and fall fast asleep.

When you wake, you are confused. You don't know where you are, but you do know that you have to go to the bathroom. Desperately. The sound of running water adds to your sense of urgency. The small round room is filled with the snores of Peter and the occasional murmuring of Dresdale. Recollection slowly percolates through your mind. Illuminated. Neila. The Desera Fox People. Caves and tunnels. MOM AND DAD ARE MISSING! Your gut clenches in anxiety. You suppress it, moving toward the sound of running water.

A tiny alcove has a wall with water spouting out of it. The water bounces and arcs across the room in an intricate pattern before disappearing down a drain. You aren't sure if it is a fountain, a toilet, a shower, or a combination of the three, but you disrobe and enter the spray of water.

Dust and weariness wash off. The water is warm but not hot and it has a strange smell and texture, as if it were part oil. Not knowing where else to go, you relieve yourself in the fountain shower and hope you haven't done something terribly wrong.

"Hey! Hurry up in there! I really gotta go!" Peter yells from outside the alcove.

"Hold on!" you reply, and out of some small spite or pettiness, you take a few extra minutes putting your clothes back on. They are dirty and smelly, but it's too cold to go naked.

"Hey! Where's the toilet?" Peter yells from the alcove.

"Just make do!"

"No potty humor, thanks."

You step back into the pod and sit on your little bed.

"Well, he certainly seems to have woken up on the sunny side of the street," Dresdale says with a yawn. Her eyes are puffy, but she doesn't look like the zombie she was the day before.

"How are you, Dres?"

"Better, I think. This whole thing has been so strange; I don't know what to make of it all. Even now it feels like a dream. Like we will wake up back at school and everything, everything will be the same. Normal. I don't know. Other times I don't want it to end. As if our other life was the dream. As if what we are doing now is the only time we'll have a chance to actually DO something. Does that sound crazy?"

"No," you reply, wanting to cry. "It doesn't sound crazy at all. I don't know what to make of it either. Sometimes it seems like a dream, but mostly it is a nightmare that I can't wake up from."

"It'll be okay," Dresdale says comfortingly. She flaps her arms helplessly, like a baby bird. "We got Neila home. We'll find your parents, too. Things will be okay."

After what seems like a long time, Peter pokes his head inside the pod.

"What's for breakfast?" he asks brightly, now that he's achieved his goal. "I'm starving."

Once again, you are amazed at Peter's ability to look fresh

and neat, even in spelunking clothes that have been abused like they were in a detergent commercial. You doubt that you look half as well-scrubbed. Your belly growls its agreement with Peter's sentiment, though, and you all laugh. The laughter feels good, even if it is a bit forced. Nerves, it's all about nerves.

"Nothing to eat in here besides our bed-moss, and as tempting as it may sound, I bet there is something better to be found!"

Peter leads the way outside and you and Dresdale follow him. You realize how you have missed the old Peter. Ever since he became Neila's de facto caregiver his good humor seemed to have drained out of him. Now, he scoots behind a rock and comes out balancing a wooden tray on the palm of his hand like a waiter in a restaurant.

"Jackpot! Look what your great benefactor has bestowed upon you lowly peons!" Peter says pompously, placing the tray on the ground and gesturing to you to take a seat. You see there are more of the gourds and a lumpy mass in a bowl that you assume is some sort of cereal.

"Don't know what it is, but it was good!" Peter says after the three of you have devoured the contents of the breakfast tray. "Kinda spicy, kinda nutty, but all good!"

"Just like you," Dresdale remarks, "but you are more spacey than spicy!"

"That's not what the other girls think!"

"Um, what other girls?"

"Yeah!"

"You know, other girls, like, from home, or town..."

"When would you get to meet girls from town?" Dresdale

asks suspiciously. "We are supposed to be on campus most of the time, well, until recently, and we haven't met one single girl since we left."

"For your information, Miss Know-It-All, I got to know quite a few girls in town while taking care of my car. They didn't seem to think I was spacey at all!" Peter says with a huff as he moves out of the pod. Dresdale looks at you with the classic 'what did I do?' look.

"Not sure," you say as you follow Peter out of the pod. "He's always been a bit sensitive about his masculine appeal, or lack thereof. I'll go see what's up."

You search around the pod that you slept in last night, but there is no sign of Peter. There are a few other house-pods on the ledge with yours, but they are all empty. You see a number of strange objects that look like a combination of dog toys and folk-art mobiles hanging from the ceiling of one of the pods, but you decide not to investigate further.

For one thing, it might be considered rude to snoop in other people's abodes. Also, you still have no idea where Peter is, so you climb back down the steep path to the pool.

Peter is not by the pool, so you explore the path that the Illuminated took Neila down. The path twists and turns and you come to a cleft in the red rock that opens into a natural amphitheater. Inside is a swarm of Illuminated surrounding a four-post tent. You guess that there are ten or twelve of the Illuminated packed around the tent. They wear simple white tunics of a shimmering cloth. Set up underneath the tent is a platform with bier. On that bier lies Neila. He seems uncon-scious. Peter is there, holding Neila's hand, and he is obviously concerned with the state of his little friend.

Peter sees you, gently releases Neila's hand and pushes through the small crowd of Illuminated. They sing some words to you, but since you left the crystal back in your sleeping pod, you can't make sense of it. Peter reaches you and moves back up the path. You glance again at the still form of Neila and see that one of the Illuminated has both of its little hands on Neila's head. Unlike any other Illuminated that you have seen, this one pulses with a deep, baleful red that reminds you of sunsets and blood. You shiver involuntarily and follow after Peter, catching up to him at the pool of clear water.

"What's happening? Is Neila going to be alright?" you ask. "That red Illuminated guy—I've never seen one that color before. What was he doing?"

"He's trying to draw the sickness, or 'mind poison,' out of Neila," Peter responds, idly flicking pebbles into the pool. "I don't know if it's just witch-doctoring or true medicine, I mean, not like our medicine, but effective. At least Neila was awake when I first saw him. He said he is feeling a bit better, but still feels really weak, as if something is sucking the life-force out of him. Anyway, they think they can revive him, just not as quickly as they'd first hoped."

"What's up with you and Dresdale?" you ask, trying to change the subject to something besides Peter's obsession with Neila's health. "You two have been butting heads a lot lately."

"Yeah, I've been a grouch, I know, but you know how it is when you're stressed. You take it out on the ones you care about the most. Besides, I can't believe she likes a dork like Garrity."

"She said it was just a crush."

"Sure, but it still made me mad. What could she see in a guy like him? Granted, he's got the football captain thing, and he is a pretty-boy, but he is so mean to the younger students. Also, he's so dumb that he would've failed History if Mrs. Trenton hadn't let him do some stupid extra credit on the history of football. The history of football! Talk about a joke."

"Why do you care? It sounds like you have a crush on her," you say without thinking.

"Maybe. Maybe I do."

You almost fall into the pool.

"Really?"

"Yeah, I guess I didn't even realize it until you asked. But this whole thing with Neila has made me get in touch with my feelings and my emotions in a way that I never have before. Look, I don't know if it is anything serious, maybe I'm just going through a phase or something, but I think I'm falling in love with Dres."

"Love?" you reply stupidly. "Love. Wow."

"Don't you dare breathe a word of this to her," Peter says, turning to you and fixing you with an intense stare. "I mean it. I shouldn't have said anything, and I will never forgive you if you say anything to her. Promise me!"

"I promise," you say automatically. You quickly turn the conversation back to Neila, your parents, the strange world you find yourself in, and other important, non-romantic topics. By the time you finish your conversation, you feel almost as if a giant ball of lead had not been poured into your belly. Almost.

"What do you mean we have to stay here for a week, or longer!" you shout at the glowing Illuminated before you— the one who had been glowing red while trying to draw the 'mind poison' out of Neila. Its name is Relevart. They don't have gender in the Illuminated colony in the same way as humans do. Peter still refers to Neila as a 'he' but there is no real basis in fact for that gender designation.

"I am sorry," Relevart sings. The crystal translates for you. You wear the translation crystal around your neck on a string. Peter has started to learn the Illuminated song-language on his own, and Dresdale is so busy checking out the features of the crystal caves that she does not need it often. "We are not warriors or traders like the Desera or the Lemurians, we are guides in the spiritual sense, not the literal. Truly we wish to help you in your quest, Child of the Child, you are known to us, and loved, but for now we must devote all of our effort to saving our light-sibling, Neila."

"Fine, we'll set off on our own then," you answer, trying to keep the anger out of your voice, and not succeeding. Even the singing translation coming from the crystal sounds angry, like a New Age artist playing death metal on a harp and pan pipes.

"That would be foolish," Relevart says. "You have seen some of the dangers in this world. Here within the bosom of the colony, you are safe. Out in the high desert of the field, you would not last long without protectors or guides."

"We could go back to the Lake of Dreams, we know the way."

"You would not make it. The Desera provided you with much protection. Just being with them kept many threats from coming at you. I am sorry. When next our friends of the Desera come, later in the week, they will take you to meet with the Lemurians in Lighthome. Be patient."

You stalk away without saying anything more. The crystal translates your silence as a high-pitched hum and you are glad to get outside. Waiting around has never been your favorite thing, and you feel like you have already done more than enough. Your skin itches with the desire to get going. It feels instinctual, like you were programmed to keep moving, just as birds migrate without ever being taught.

Peter is no help. "Look," he says. "Relevart and the others have put us up and are feeding us; they are doing a lot already. Besides, they said the Desera would be back at the end of the week. I saw something big and scaly flying over the plain this morning. You, me, and Dres all need a break, and I have to be here to look after Neila."

You open your mouth, and before the words, comes regret, and then the words.

"I didn't know you came to help Neila, I thought you came to help me."

"I wouldn't be here if I weren't trying to help."

"Where would you be then? Where else would you go?" You don't go any further, you don't say 'You're an orphan, you have no home.' But Peter and you both know that is what you mean. Peter's lip curls back, as if to smile, but it is not a smile.

"I don't know, but I am here now. I'll ignore what you just said. I don't want you to have to go through what I have, so that is what I am trying to prevent. Don't forget that. Also don't forget that rushing off into that crazy red desert without help will do one of two things, kill you quickly, or kill you slowly."

"Thank you for all of your help," you say stiffly. You do mean the thanks, but you are still too angry for the words to come out the way you mean. The crystal hums and you want to throw it away. Instead you take it from around your neck and gently toss it to Peter. "You can have the translation crystal, so you can talk to Neila all you want."

"I don't need it," he replies, tossing it back to you.

You hold the hissing crystal in your hand and walk out of the pod.

Taking a swim in the pool helps your mood, and you start to realize what a jerk you have been. You go back to your temporary home and tell Peter you are sorry for what you said.

"Don't worry about it," he replies, but his eyes are tight.

Over the next few days you and Peter just ignore your fight, as if everything was fine, but you both know it isn't. Peter spends more time with Relevart and Neila. You feign interest in Neila's health status and daily updates on his care, but it's obvious to everyone that your true interest lies ahead.

Since Dresdale is consumed by work in the caves, and Peter is with Neila all day, you quickly decide that you need something to occupy yourself or you'll go crazy. Relevart introduces you to an Illuminated named Ediug, who brings you out into the scrubland and desert.

He teaches you that the large, scaly thing Peter saw is a flying reptile scavenger called a "crushbeak." You learn that the translation is literal when Ediug takes you near the rotting carcass of an enormous camel and you watch as the crushbeaks break into the huge thigh bones of the dead animal.

Ediug shows you many other secrets of the inner desert: where to find water, which plants are edible by humans, and how to navigate based on shadow movements. You grow to respect and enjoy the presence of Ediug, but the itch to do something, anything, persists, and seems to get stronger.

Then you get the bad news.

"The Desera will not be here this week," Relevart tells you. "I am sorry to tell you this; I know that you have been waiting for their arrival. They will try to be here two weeks from now, but they may not be able to make it even then. Sceptus has broken through the Lemurian defenses. He controls all the main travel routes into and out of the inner desert. Again, I am sorry."

Relevart bows to you, and you appreciate the gesture. This time, you are in control of yourself.

"Thank you, Relevart, for all you have done, both for me and for my friends. We appreciate the hospitality that you have shown us. I will work with Ediug to help bring in as many resources as possible to help repay your generosity." This time the crystal sings, but you are filled with despair.

"You brought Neila to us, and for that we are in debt to you. We do not forget."

"Please let me know if they can get here any sooner," you say as you leave the darkness of the cave. As always when you leave the still darkness, you are startled by the noise and brightness outside of that cave. You head back to the pod and grab your towel.

"Mind if I join you?" Dresdale asks, looking up from a borrowed book from The Illuminated.

"Sure," you reply, trying not to make the same sort of mistake as the last time you were delayed. Dresdale didn't appreciate being teased about her crush, and you think part of that teasing was from your disappointment. Also, you feel different, sensing that maybe a decision has been made and you are just waiting to learn about it. Somehow you know you are not going to wait another two weeks, no matter what.

Dresdale spares you any conversation on the way down and while you swim your laps, and you appreciate the quiet. After a good swim, you both pull up on the sunny side of the pool and perch on the rocks like monkeys. Instead of fur, you have towels, but they are meant for The Illuminated, so they are a little small for you.

"How are you doing?" you ask, trying to be a good friend. "Can you imagine what your parents are thinking? They must be frantic."

"They'll be fine," Dresdale responds breezily. "I left them that message saying I was okay. Besides, I don't know how to get in touch with them. I asked Relevart, but he said all of The Illuminated are in the Inner Earth now. He said he would ask the Lemurians, but no word yet. There is one other thing that is bothering me though."

"What's that?"

"Peter is such a grouch to me lately. He is constantly giving me grief about one thing or another."

"Like what?" you ask, not having been aware of the friction between Peter and Dresdale.

"Well, when I was going down to come swimming the yesterday, he was staring at me, and when I looked up at him, he laughed."

"Maybe he was laughing about something else."

"Well, then he said, 'That is one ugly looking swimming costume! Even the Victorians would have laughed.' I know I look stupid wearing this little shirt from the Illuminated and my hiking shorts, but still..."

"That doesn't sound that bad, besides, maybe he was staring at you for another reason and got embarrassed when you caught him."

"It's not just that, it's other things, too. Like when I make any noise when I'm translating, he'll start trying to imitate it. It's really starting to bug me."

"Look, he's a guy, and guys do stupid, annoying things sometimes. Maybe he just doesn't know any other way to show his interest."

Dresdale's head snaps around and she stares straight at you.

"What do you mean 'interest'?"

You freeze. Did you just spill the beans? Or did you merely open the bag a crack, and can easily snap it shut?

"Hel-lo? I said, what do you mean 'interest'?"

The sun has now slipped behind the mountains, and you start to shiver.

If you choose to cover it up with a little backtracking, turn to page 163.

If you decide that you have already given the secret away, and tell Dresdale about Peter's crush, turn to page 157.

Finger in the Clouds

J ust take it then and let's get out of here!"

Tat shrugs, lifts the sack and bundle and slides out of the door in one smooth motion. You follow, feeling like a thief.

Tat moves carefully at first, staying to the darker spots, but then breaks into a run as soon as you are away from the houses of the small town. You reach Noaaon to find him conscious and sitting up. Tat brews the herbs in a small pot over a campstove made from a finely-tooled rock filled with dry needles from the trees sheltering you. They crackle and pop.

Noaaon perks up almost immediately after drinking the pungent-smelling mixture of fungus, leaves, and powder. "We go now," he says, standing up and swaying. Still, he manages to continue at a faster pace than the three of you "surfaceworlders." Tat drives you until you literally collapse to the ground. You cut your hands on the sharp rocks of the animal path that she leads you over when you fall. Dresdale helps you clean the bigger pieces of dirt from the wounds. All Peter can do is gasp and try and find a breath that is not there.

"Never do I want to feel like this again," he wheezes after a few minutes of rest. "Even 'Hell Week' at soccer practice didn't come close to this."

"War. Be strong," Tat says, throwing some of the dried mushrooms that you took from the farmhouse. The fungus tastes so good in your mouth that you can't believe it. It tastes like the richest, most perfect truffle you could ever imagine, the only quibble being its dryness. You gulp a drink from Tat's canteen and the flavors explode in your mouth.

"'Stolen fruit is twice as sweet,'" Dresdale says after trying the mushrooms. Suddenly the taste is not as wondrous in your mouth. "Of course, having run throughout the night might have something to do with it too. You know, the 'top of the mountain effect,' 'hunger is the best sauce,' and all that. How far do you think we ran tonight?"

"Too far," Peter answers with a groan. "Way too far. But if I had to guess, I would say ten miles or so, over rough ground. Not to mention our packs."

"At least we're not sick," you add, looking over at Noaaon. He is shaking and mumbling to himself as Tat prepares more of the tea. His face looks drawn and pale in the light from the now brightening speck of sun.

Tat made camp high up another cliff, but this one had an almost regular staircase hidden behind a nearly invisible door made from the cliff rock. "Trogs," is her only explanation when Dresdale asks who made it. The steps are uncomfortably spaced for your legs, but you can tell that whoever carved this hideout knew what they were doing. A small landing on the outside of the cliff provides a well-concealed viewing spot of the landscape that stretches out before you.

"Kind of like a bowl that doesn't end," Peter offers when he takes his turn peering out over the valley. "Everything about this place is so weird! But kind of familiar, like Utah or Arizona or someplace, what with the trees and stuff and the farmhouses and that town over there. But even if I had never been to Utah or Arizona, I would know that this was not it."

Turn to page 47.

Falling Crystal

It's clearly a trap," you say with conviction. "But even if it isn't, I'm not sure that going to the heart of the empire would make sense."

"We have few resources or assets in the capital of New Babel. Lemurians are not welcome there anymore. A few remember the time when we were not considered vermin or vampires, but mostly they are old, poorly connected, or both," Durno explains with a weary sadness. "I'll go and tell Prince Torgan that you will join the expedition to the Great Cave. You should all sleep. We leave in the morning."

"You're coming?" you ask, relief too obvious in your voice.

"Someone needs to watch over you youngsters, and it may as well be me until we find Rimy." Durno likes to think of himself as almost outer-earth human, at least part of the time.

You, Peter, and Dresdale follow the tall Lemurian assigned to show you your room. It seems you will be staying on the island castle. Your room is small, clean, and chilly. A wash basin in the corner has hot and cold running water, and thick fluffy towels that smell like dried moss. The four cots jammed in the room take up most of the floor space. Your few possessions fit under the beds.

Washing your face and hands with warm water is a luxury that you had not really appreciated fully before. You watch the red dust swirl down the drain as you clean your face and neck.

"Time is up," Peter says, tapping you on the shoulder. "We may go where you go, but you don't get to hog the sink. What if the hot water runs out?"

"Don't even say such a horrible thing!" Dresdale says.

You move out of the way and pick up one of the moss towels. The water disappears so quickly, you wonder if the moss might still be alive and drinking it up.

"You know, I never did ask you two what you wanted to do," you say. "I'm sorry about that."

"Well, I wanted to go on the expedition, and I thought Durno was right. Peter might have thought differently though."

Peter moves out of the way for Dresdale and picks up one of the towels. "It's okay. I think we made the right choice, but when you think about what has been happening to us, it all seems a little too much."

"Yeah, no kidding. How do we turn this light off? I need to sleep."

You dream of mother. You dream of father. You dream of home.

You cross back over the wire bridge in the morning, but return is easier somehow. Prince Torgan rallies his expeditionary force in the grey stone courtyard. They look professional to you. Ropes, harnesses, and what you take to be local versions of crampons, pitons, and other rock climbing supplies take up the most part of the two powered carts that the Lemurians have set up. They also have four animal cages made of the same translucent wire as the bridge. Two of the cages hold what you would have thought of as large bats before the other night. The other two smaller cages hold two lizards. The bats seem to be sleeping amidst the clamor of the preparations, but the lizards watch you with unblinking eyes.

"Where are we going?" you ask one of your traveling companions in stuttering Lemurian. You are not sure at first if they understood you.

The Lemurian looks up at you and answers, but all you catch is the word "Kringto" because she repeats it three times for you after seeing the confused look on your face.

"I think that is the word for 'volcano'," Dresdale says.

"Wonderful, just wonderful."

"Hey, at least we have done some spelunking when we were at the Carlsbad dig last summer. We might be even able to show Durno a thing or two!"

"Yeah, but that was in a cave, Peter, not a freakin' volcano."

You notice the Prince motioning everyone to get ready to move out. A low-slung flatbed truck rolls into the courtyard, and the other members of your party start loading the powered carts and the loose bags onto it. You all help. Within minutes, everything is loaded onto the truck, including the members of the party.

"Good luck on your journey!" Prince Torgan says. The translation crystal has been set up in the courtyard. "Follow the Emerald Warrior to the place where the soul is filled. We need to find Orana to fulfill the return of the emerald shard. We are strong, but we need the help of Orana to bring all the peoples of this world together. You are the keys to unlocking the doors of cooperation and survival. Go with luck and haste!"

"We'll take this truck all the way to the Lake of Clouds," Durno announces as you roll out of the courtyard. The side of the truck extends to the ground. You can't tell how you are moving forward. "After that, we'll have to head cross-country through the foothills until we come to the Kringto. It should take us at least two weeks."

"Two weeks!" you shout. "Tell me again that the rumor of my parents was a trap, Durno, because right now two weeks could mean the difference between life and death for them!"

"This is necessary, and yes, it was most definitely a trap. Sceptus will do anything to get you. You are the Emerald Warrior, and as such, a threat."

"How does he know about me?"

"Too many people know about you. He knows. Everyone knows."

You think about that as you ride. The speed is disconcerting as you move along the red road. Someone out there had kidnapped your parents and most likely was laying traps for you. Everyone was saying it was Emperor Sceptus, but so far no one had any proof. You let your mind go blank. Thoughts bang around, wanting your attention, but you ignore them. Who can be trusted? The trouble is that life on the upper world isn't much better.

Durno distributes lunch to everyone and has quick words with several individuals. This time lunch is a soft cheese with a creamy and sour aftertaste, coupled with hard black bread. Your party consists of eight Lemurians, your two friends, and yourself. Turina is with you, but Keldso was sent back to the camp where you first docked.

You estimate that you have been traveling at about sixty miles an hour. Near day's end, when the sun starts to dim, Durno brings the truck to a halt.

"Time to earn our living," he says, jumping off the back of the truck. "There is our goal, Kringto, in the distance." He points to a distant cone with a broken tip that towers over all the mountains and volcanoes around it. A thin trail of smoke trickles out of the top into the redness of a soot-filled sky.

"You will be okay," says Turina to the three of you as you stare at the distant volcano. "This time we get to ride!"

She hops up onto one of the powered carts and motions the three of you to do the same. When you do, a Lemurian presses his finger on the side of the cart. It slowly rises from the edge of the flatbed and hovers in the air with you and your gear. The Lemurian grabs a handle on the edge of the cart and pushes you off the truck to the edge of the road. He jogs up a narrow path between rock faces. You try not to look down as you climb through narrow passes, but going down is worse.

Your trip is not exactly a free ride. All of you take your turns pushing the cart. When you and Dresdale take your turns, Peter cracks himself up by making "hyah!" noises and yelling "mush," "haw," and "gee" as much as possible. At first you laugh along with him, but the novelty fades quickly. Your muscles ache.

For the next ten days you push the hovering carts through the mountains. You are thankful for the ample water supply that you have brought. Your muscles become stiff and sore from all the running. Durno sees that the three of you are tired. He allows you a brief rest. You see him rummaging through a black back, and then he calls you over. He has a special cream for your legs.

"What made you join up with Sublimas-Chaeko?" you ask him as you rub the cream in. Immediately your legs feel better. "This stuff is great! We could have used that on our soccer team!"

"I wanted to be a poet-gatherer," Durno says quietly, "but I was little then. This was before, when Sceptus hadn't spread his lies about us. After he started his war of words against us Lemurians, my father joined with Sublimas-Chaeko. I joined him when I grew old enough."

"What is a poet-gatherer?" you ask.

"A poet-gatherer brings words and ideas to different people. These words are clumsy for me and I am not explaining it correctly, but it is like being a spreader of truth. Maybe I will get a chance in the future-life, but not now. Each day I fight to do what my father would want me to. I don't know if he would be proud or not."

Dresdale fills a notebook that she got in Lighthome with drawings of the mountains and the few signs of life in this arid and rocky land. "Look! The pages are made from a special insect secretion that the Lemurians harvest!"

"I know," Peter says conspiratorially, "we'll get the recipe and market it Earthside! Bug Spit Paper! We can't lose."

When you get close to the volcano, Durno brings the party together to give you more information. "The cave itself is hard to access. There are three main chambers to the Great Cave. They were formed when a huge bubble of magma built up below the volcano. It grew so slowly that the outside of it hardened as it expanded. When it finally started leaking from the bottom, a hollow interior with three lobes was left behind. Lava tunnels lead inward and connect the Great Cave to the limestone network that eventually connects to the Troglodyte kingdom. Theoretically you can reach the cave where Orana is through the Trog tunnels, but the only reliable directions we have go through the Great Cave."

"Will there be anyone else in the Great Cave?"

"You never know," Durno says. "This land is too harsh to support a permanent settlement, but since it is a holy place, there are sometimes pilgrims or others who come. The cave is seen as representing the inner world within the inner world."

"Okay, let's get to this Russian nesting doll of a place," Peter says.

When you reach the base of the volcano the huge bubble of the Great Cave looms above you. The dark grey of the hardened lava stands out against the red background, but details are obscured by smoke and soot. The entrance to the Great Cave is one of the hollow lava tubes that reach out from the bubble like the legs of a spider. The black sand in front of the entrance is smoothed and scraped like that of a sand trap on a golf course. You note a large footprint that looks like it was left by a giant chicken.

The climb up through the lava tubes takes hours. You don't have to break out the climbing tools yet, as earlier visitors had put in a few steps and piled boulders to make the route passable. Everything is old and worn, but passable. You feel like you are climbing a giant's staircase.

When you finally step out into the first chamber of the Great Cave, all you see is darkness except for a tiny ray of light from your headlamp falling into nothingness. Then, indistinct, you notice specks of light, like fireflies, dancing in the darkness.

"Durno, I think there is someone else here," Dresdale says, pointing to the specks of light. The specks stop dancing. You strain to see more clearly, but you can't see anything more.

You turn to see Durno staring at the dark figure of Morphus on the far side of the cave. He runs to attack the black figure.

"Durno! Don't go near him!!" you yell. It's too late.

In an instant, the whole of the first chamber of the Great Cave is illuminated. You see the sharp interior of a hollow lava bubble. All around you, liquid stone forms are frozen into drips and flows. But your complete attention is captivated by three people standing where the specks of light were. You see Bram Interious standing with your parents! Then you hear the sound from the explosion that lit up the cave. Then you hear cries of pain from members of your group.

"What happened?" you shout, blind from the light flash.

"Run! Get out of here!"

You blink away the stars from your eyes. Your headlamp is still working—good. You turn its gaze towards Morphus, or where he was standing. Durno lies in a heap on the floor of the cave. Smoke burns upwards from his clothes. You can't tell if he is dead or just unconscious. You run forward, reach down, pick him up and run for the entrance tunnel. Everyone else has gone ahead, but Dresdale waits for you and helps you carry him.

You round a corner and set Durno down. He is not moving. You remove his face shield. His eyes are closed.

"He's dead," says Dresdale. Her face is pale beneath the red grime, and tears run down her face. But her voice is strong.

Turina moves forward and gently lays her hands on Durno's unmoving face. Keldso starts to moan. A flash of blue light comes out of Turina's hands.

"Oh my god! What is she doing?!" Peter screams. He points at Turina. She holds Durno's lifeless head between her two hands. Small blue sparks dance over his body, and you see it turning into vapor before you. Soon there is nothing left but dust, and a small clear crystal that falls into Turina's hands.

"She, she, absorbed his body!" Dresdale shouts. "Oh my god, he faded away like a ghost!"

Turina turns to you, holding the crystal forward.

"Durno," is all she says before running back the way you came.

You look to the area where your parents were standing with Bram Interious. Were they really there, or was it just an illusion?

"How did they know we were going to be here?" Peter asks,

grabbing you by the arm and pulling. Dresdale takes your other arm and then pulls you away from the scene of the explosion, the scene of Durno's death. The crystal pulses in your hand. Your heart pounds. You want to scream, but you hold it in.

"Pick up your legs and move them!" Peter shouts at you. You are tired of shouting. You want to sit down.

"You're not Durno! Stop ordering me around!"

"Durno's dead! You're going to be next unless you get moving!"

"I think I'm in shock," you reply, but somehow you manage to move.

"We all are. Keep moving!"

You exit the Great Cave and look down at your carts. They are surrounded by soldiers. A dirigible trailing a streamer of exploding lines crawls across the sky. Lizards and their riders fly down from above.

"Oh man, we cannot catch a break!" Peter groans.

"We have to go back in!"

You take a deep breath, steady yourself, and go back inside the darkness of the Great Cave. It has gone back to being dark, calm, and soothing, settling on you like a cloak. Your forehead pulses. You take a deep breath.

"Follow me, I know where to go," you say, leading your friends deeper and deeper into the cave.

Continues in *The Golden Path: Volume III, Paying the Ferryman.*

Continued from page 51.

Finger in the Clouds

W hen is the next 'public ceremony'?" Dresdale asks, "and how is it that you speak English so well? Certainly it can't be the native language in this place."

"Five days from now, the fleet of flying ships will be named and given to the gods and to Sceptus. All will be gathered in the triumphal square for the rally. So many thousands of people will be there. It is required."

"Could you please answer my other question?" Dres is trying hard to sound polite and not nosy.

"Yes, it is the court language. I worked there in my youth, for your blessed grandmother, peace be on her soul. I learned it there."

"How strange."

"We must go, even this place is not safe, come with me."

She leads you deeper into the city, and you feel as if you are traveling up the sides of a pyramid of people and machines. You travel streets swarming with people, clanging with activity, movement, and hurry. You make it two layers up towards the tower, with steep streets connecting the different steppes. Cablecars with large mechanical ferry workers in and out of the factories, farms and airship yards. Everything looks new, yet it has quickly become dirty, blackened by the soot blasting out of the smokestacks.

Marta leads you to a small apartment building. You are pleasantly surprised when she leads you into a small enclosed garden filled with colorful plants, flowers, and butterflies. She makes up cots on the floor of the kitchen and living room for you, but she only has two, so one of you has to sleep on a bunch of cushions put together.

"Rock smashes scissors," you inform Peter after a fierce battle, having lost the first round to Dresdale. "You are Senor Cushion tonight."

Marta does not let you out of the house for three days. She feeds you well. Her soups are amazing—sweet, sour, and satisfying, and her homemade bread is dark and flavored with a pungent fungus that gives it a lasting flavor. She leaves early in the morning, after making breakfast, and does not return until well after dark to make you dinner.

However, with no books, computers, or entertainment systems, you have to make do with conversation among yourselves or find other amusements. Dresdale finds paper and an oddly L-shaped stylus from Marta and busies herself making detailed notes on all that she can discern about the various things she has seen so far.

You and Peter, left on your own, talk about how you will contact your parents, what you'll say, and then start over. You alternate that with old gossip from school, analysis of Tat, Noaaon, Marta, Ama, and the others you have met so far.

"I am going to scream if I have to stay inside much longer," you threaten at the end of the third day.

"Please spare us," Dresdale says without looking up from

her pile of papers. She seems to be drawing a depiction of the tower, reaching toward a sky that is a looming presence hanging above.

Turn to page 11.

Farmhouse

Neither choice sounds appealing," you explain to Ama, "but I feel that any delay could be, I don't know, a disaster somehow..." Your voice trails off and you look to Dresdale and Peter for support.

"Hey, we're going to be okay," Peter says, picking up the burden of being positive. "I managed to get Lieutenant McMann to throw in a bunch of those energy bars. They taste like rehydrated coprolites, but they'll help us make it."

"How did you learn the name for fossilized feces?" Dresdale asks Peter with amazement. He just smiles.

"Any extra food will certainly help your chances. I will arrange for the scouts and soldiers who will accompany you on your journey," Ama says with a smile.

"Once we are there, assuming we make it, then what?"

"In New Babel we have a group of Agarthans who support the rightful ruler of the land. That ruler is your mother," she says, looking at you. "She has been gone for many years, but the people remember her, and her mother, your grandmother, Empress Bellatria Hinstrider. Sceptus may have forced your grandmother to marry him, but many chafed under the rule of the foreigner. They will help you once you get to New Babel."

"What are you talking about?!" you shout at Ama. "This makes no sense. My mom is Dutch, not some princess from the Inner Earth!"

"You can choose not to believe, but it does not change the truth."

"Fine. Let's just say that my mom is some sort of cave princess or something. Or maybe people just think she is. Ever hear of Anastasia Romanov? Anyway, I'll deal with that later. Please continue. I'm sorry about my outburst, but I'm tired and worried."

"Of course I understand," Ama says formally, before continuing, "but you will have to understand as well. There are many forces at work here. Old forces, old grudges, and new terrors. You need to be careful. Rest tonight. You will leave at first brightening."

Your mind swirls with disbelief and exhaustion. Exhaustion wins out and you collapse into sleep on the thin wooden bed with its woven straw mat.

"Okay muchachos, we have to hit it," Peter says with the vigor of a camp counselor.

You stuff your gear into your bag with your eyes half-closed and struggle to fully wake up. You know you need to be alert for this journey. Dresdale seems to be in the same state as you, and you take comfort in her companionship.

Ama meets you at the cave exit with the scouts and soldiers who will guide and protect you. However, there is only one of each, not the five you were expecting. Ama notices your surprise.

"With limited food, I made the decision that we would keep the party as small as possible. Tat will be your scout," Ama says, pointing to a tall woman with long dark hair and a stern face. "She knows the way to New Babel, and all its dangers. Noaaon is a blooded warrior with coup," Ama continues, pointing at the short, dark man with long hair held in a ponytail. He has a long, curved knife sheathed at his side, and a small bow made of horn hung over his shoulder. "Pay attention to them, they are all the protection you have in a dangerous world."

"Thank you," you say to Ama. Tat and Noaaon have already left the cave and are in the first light of the inner world sun's daily brightening. You leave the cool darkness of the cave, and you feel naked and vulnerable in the sere desert landscape of this strange world. However, you have little time to contemplate the strangeness, that is, if you want to keep up with your escorts.

"Do you think they would just leave us behind?" Peter asks, panting. Your guides are disappearing around the corner of a large boulder on the ridgeline that you are traversing.

"Probably not," Dresdale answers, also panting from the pace, "but let's not find out!"

You camp in a small cave high up the side of a cliff as the sun speck dims at the end of a long day. Shaky legs and arms make the climb up the stone steps carved in the rock tricky. Peter has to steady you once from behind when your sweaty hand slips off the smooth rock.

"Thanks, buddy," you whisper.

"De nada."

The view from the cave is stunning. Light glints off the Sea of Tears with a purple glare that is almost blinding, but the most astonishing sight is the way the world just keeps going up and up into the sky, until it all fades into a brownish-red haze of distance.

Tat and Noaaon make a simple dinner of water, dried fruit, and jerky of some sort. Dresdale tries to be polite in refusing the meat, but your guides don't seem to care, and they split and eat Dresdale's portion without expression. Unfortunately, they don't give her any extra dried fruit.

The next day is much like the first, but more painful, as you are sore. By the time you get your dried fruit, meat, and water, you eat it so quickly your stomach hurts.

"Those two don't seem to care for us very much," Peter whispers to you during a break at the hottest point of the day. The five of you are crouched under the lip of a rock overhang.

"I think it might be the language barrier," Dresdale whispers back.

"Sure, that's part of it," Peter replies, "but I get the sense that they just want to get rid of us."

"Of course they do!" you interject. "Isn't it obvious? Those two are pros, and they don't like having to babysit a bunch of kids on half-rations. We head into Agarthan territory tomorrow. We'll have to watch ourselves."

"I am not a kid!" Peter hisses at you. "I may be young, but I am not a kid!"

"Chill! I mean to them you are, not to me."

Tat and Noaaon mime and demonstrate the proper techniques for hiding in the scrub of the foothills. They give you thin jackets of fine cloth that blend almost perfectly with the colors of the landscape.

"Stay still," Tat says. It is her favorite thing to say, but most times she just gives you a hard look, meaning the same thing.

Noaaon looks over at the three of you and snorts dismissively. He and Tat talk for a bit, and then they look at you again. It makes you very uncomfortable. They move forward slowly, looking around in every direction.

"Agartha," Tat tells you at one point during the morning.

You can't tell the difference visually between the place you just were and where you are now, but it does feel different somehow. An electric thrill courses through you, like that beside a rushing stream, or a mountaintop, but more intense. Gradually you notice the landscape change as you creep through it. It all flattens out a bit, and the soil seems richer. Thick mosses, dark green and blue, come to dominate the area. The dampness in the air soothes you, but Tat and Noaaon seem even more agitated than you have seen them before.

You camp in a grotto that is hidden and secure. Even there your native companions don't relax. So far you have not seen anyone. You have crossed three roads. Peter deemed them "glorified goat paths."

The next day, you see a small village in the distance. Except for the strange moss, the red light, the smell, taste and feel of the land you are in, it could almost be home. Real trees with blue needles strive upward to the red sun, while gigantic mushrooms feed on the fallen in the dark corners of the folded land.

You make camp in the midst of a blowdown. A small stream flows nearby, and you guzzle the clear, cold water until you can't fill yourself anymore and your lips are practically numb. You wash the dirt of the trail off your face and you watch it float away.

"We're out of food," Peter tells you. You already knew, but you were half-pretending that you didn't. Your belly rumbles loudly at the mention of food. No one laughs.

"Let's go to sleep," you say, "hopefully we'll find something to eat in the morning."

"Ooooahhhh!"

"Wha-what's that?" you stutter, shocked into wakefulness by the strange noise. By the light of the dimmed sun peeking through thin clouds, you see that Noaaon is writhing on the ground. Foam is coming out of his mouth.

"I think he's having a seizure," Dresdale says calmly.

Tat grabs him and holds him down until the seizure passes, but Noaaon doesn't regain consciousness and his face twists in pain on a regular basis. You, Tat, Peter, and Dresdale take care of him during the day, but he looks weaker and weaker as time goes by.

"We need to get him medicine, food," you say to Tat after Noaaon gives a particularly sad moan.

"I know," she answers, looking worried and human. Surprisingly, her English has improved rapidly during the day. So rapidly that you worry about some of the things you may have said in front of her and Noaaon. "We must go to the village. We can get what we need. Now, we go."

"You sure we should leave Noaaon here without someone to watch out for him?" Peter asks as you leave the protection of the toppled trees.

"No choice. Quiet."

You creep behind Tat towards the village. Although the land is much greener and more lush than the red desert of the Forgotten People, you are still surrounded by a harsh and rocky environment. As you get closer to town, you see tilled fields on tiny scraps of terraced earth. All of the crops have been harvested and the ground is barren except for the stalks of what was there before.

At the edge of one of the larger fields, a small farmhouse is nestled in a copse of needle trees. The trees are sort of a cross between the regular pines where you are camped and large cactus, and the round shape of the farmhouse fits well with the tubular branches of the strange trees. A thin wisp of smoke floats from the chimney into the fading light and disappears in the always crushing sky.

You wait in silence until the inner world's night has fully arrived. Tat motions you forward at that point and you follow her to the back door of the farmhouse. A lizard streaks past you as you enter the courtyard, and you almost cry out in surprise, but you manage to hold it in. Your heart beats hard.

Tat takes a thin strip of metal and deftly inserts it into the lock on the door. She bangs it hard once with her knife and the door springs open. Tat rushes in, and you, Dresdale, and Peter follow.

"Check house! Get people, kitchen!" Tat hisses at you as she sprints through the kitchen and up the stairs to the second floor. The three of you stand there, stunned and unmoving. You can't believe you just broke into someone's house.

Tat returns with a scared-looking blonde woman holding a crying baby. The woman's face is tight and white. Tat yells at her but you can't understand what she is saying. The woman shakes her head and you wonder if that actually means 'no.' It wouldn't surprise you if it meant the opposite here.

"What is she doing to that poor woman?" Dresdale asks, anger in her voice. "What are we doing here?"

"Yeah," Peter adds. "This is a pretty serious shakedown scene."

Tat seems frustrated with the woman, and she starts opening all of the cupboards and drawers, looking for food and medicine. She finds very little. The baby stops crying, but the sound of Tat searching is more unnerving in the silence.

"Bazock!" Tat finally yells, and you assume that she is cursing. "Is all them have," she adds in English, holding up a sack half-full of root vegetables and a small bag of dried mushrooms. "Little bit of medicine. Maybe not enough. Sceptus army take all food. We go."

Tat gives the woman one last hard look and gets ready to leave.

"Wait! We can't take all of her food!" Dresdale implores.

"We need," Tat replies, shifting her hard look to Dresdale. "No food, Noaaon die, you die, I die."

"Maybe we could just take half." Peter proposes, looking pained and conflicted about the whole situation. All four of you are in the grip of a hunger you have never felt before, and even the sight of the dried mushrooms and raw vegetables makes your mouth salivate in anticipation.

"Not enough. They get more. We go now!"

If you agree with Peter and take only half of the food, turn to page 7.

If you listen to Tat, and take all of the food, turn to page 129.

Black Mask

Feeling lightheaded, you scramble down the side of the ridge to the outcropping, trying to make as little noise as possible. The bats are aware of your presence, moving away from your direction. They begin clicking and grunting to each other. A simple leather ring ties the elbow of each bat's wing to a foot. They move around on their feet awkwardly.

"It's okay," you whisper, moving towards the three bats. They tower over you, and their faces look frightening up close. "I'm just here to check on you."

One of them grunts and moves closer. Reaching up, you feel for the clasp that holds the canister and controls the poison release system. You remember setting the system, but the perspective is all wrong. You remember being taller when standing next to the bat. A feeling of disassociation sweeps over you. Still you're able to focus on the task at hand and undo the harness of the canister.

The second bat moves away from you, sniffing the air furiously. Finally, you corner it against the drop-off on the far side of the outcropping. Getting the canister off the second bat takes much longer than the first. The bat's hobbled wings buffets you about the head and face and you see the first stars since you have been inside the Earth. Sweat drips off the end of your nose.

Getting the third bat's canister is still a chore, but you persevere and manage to remove it. Without pausing, you sling the three canisters over your back and hurry up the steep slope back towards camp. Exhausted as you are, you manage to scurry up the slope. Looking over your shoulder, you see that the three bats are still by themselves.

"Durno?" you whisper as you near the entrance to your shelter. You have no idea how long you have been gone, but it's still dark. No reply.

"Durno? Dres? Peter?"

No one there! But all of your gear is still there. You spin around to run. A knife-point under your nose stops you.

"Too late, you are," says the dark shape holding the knife. "Hand over the canisters."

You slowly lower the poison canisters to the ground. The knife slides down to your throat. The face of the man in front of you is hidden by a black mask of rippling cloth. The shifting movements of the mask make you dizzy. You turn away as much as possible. Something hits your head from behind and you fall to the rocky ground. How did I understand what he said? you think as you start to lose consciousness. He was speaking Agarthan!

You wake up in a cage made from long strips of flexible wood. It is suspended from the ceiling. From the shaking and the noise, you think that you are in a ship. The air is foul with the smell of sickness and filth, but you can taste the faint tang of the salt air.

Other cages swing nearby, but you don't recognize anyone. The other prisoners are ragged and thin. They lean desperately against the bars of their cages. Your cage is too short to stand upright, and too narrow to sit down. You make yourself as comfortable as possible, which is somewhere between misery and agony, and wait for your captors to return.

"Help!" You yell, but your voice is a dry croak. None of the other prisoners looks at you. "Help!"

Whack! Something hits the side of your cage and sets it spinning. As you spin, you catch a glimpse of a thin man dressed in oiled leather.

"You will have no help here!" the man roars as he sets your cage spinning in the other direction. You are so dizzy that you feel ill.

"Where are you taking me?" you say, with strange words and sounds coming from you as if you had always spoken a different language. "Where are my friends?"

The man laughs, spits, and then speaks.

"You are going to a great place, for a devil! Emperor Sceptus needs slaves to work in his sulfur pits. You are a slave. You will work in the pits."

The man in oiled leather laughs again, hits your cage once more, and walks away.

The End

Seven League Boots

O h come on," you reply, "don't tell me you can't tell!" In for a penny...

"What EXACTLY do you mean?" Dresdale says, turning to face you and giving you a look that makes you think twice.

"You know what I mean. The stupid jokes. How he always is hovering near you, as awkward as a freshman at the big dance. It is sort of pathetic, acting like he's a kindergartner and that by being mean to you he'll get more attention. As I said before, guys act like idiots sometimes... "

"This is really serious," Dresdale says, her face looking pained. "You don't think he, you know, likes me? Do you?"

"Yeah, that is what I mean, it's so obvious." As you say it you worry that you may have gone too far. Scratch that, you know you have gone too far. If Peter finds out that you betrayed his confidence he will be furious, or something worse than that.

"Do NOT tell him that I told you," you say to Dresdale.

"I won't," Dres says distractedly. "You're sure that he isn't just joking or something? Maybe you are just seeing things. Maybe you just don't understand what Peter is really thinking. I'm sure that is all it is."

"Well, he told me as much, so I don't think that I am seeing things that aren't there." Stop, you tell yourself. You have gone too far, but something in you wants to keep going too far. It might be jealousy, but you don't spend the time to make sure before continuing with the words that will drive a wedge deep into the heart of your tripartite friendship. A friendship that started years before and has withstood the storms of growing from children to almost-adults. Almost adults. "He told me that he likes you, you know, romantically."

"Oh no, that's horrible!"

"You have to PROMISE me right now, that you won't breathe a word of this to Peter. He would be so angry at me. You have to promise!"

"Okay, okay, I promise!" Dresdale says hotly before adding in a more subdued tone, "how long have you known?"

"Just a couple of days, but I was starting to get an idea or two back at school."

"How come you didn't tell me?!"

"Well, I'm telling you now!"

"Thanks a lot!"

You walk back to the sleeping pod in silence. Regret fills your soul. No good will come of this, you think. You hope that Dres doesn't babble like you just did.

"Remember, you promised, just act normal!" you whisper urgently before you enter the pod.

"Of course!"

"Hey guys, have a nice swim?" Peter asks when you enter.

"Yeah, it was great, you should come next time," you answer, hearing yourself sounding normal.

"Yeah, I'm just bushed from helping Neila, maybe next time. What's up with you, Dres? Why are you staring at me like that?"

"Oh, nothing," Dresdale says, blushing. Her skin turns so pink that most of her freckles disappear. "Uh, sorry."

"No worries. I'm going to hit it."

Even after the lamp is turned down low, you stay awake.

The next day passes pretty normally. Dresdale works on translating tablets ("Some of these might be a hundred thousand years old or more! Can you believe that?!"), Peter helps Neila ("I think he's really coming around!"), you bug Relevart and spend the rest of the day catching yellow frogs with Ediug in a cistern-like pond hidden deep within the red rocks of the desert ("Pay attention, they have a nasty bite, so always grab them from behind, and always leave at least twenty to repopulate the colony!").

The next day things start to fall apart.

"Jeez, Dres, were you born on Planet Clumsy?" Peter teases when Dresdale drops a tablet on the floor. "Or was it Planet Tabulus Dropus?!" He laughs at her expense.

"Very nice, Peter!" Dresdale snaps. "I don't know how you think your being mean will ever make me like you!"

You swallow hard. Peters face looks scared for a long moment. Then his old grin reappears, but with a slight brittleness to it. "Don't flatter yourself, Dres, you're not my type."

"Whatever, play your stupid little kindergartner games, but

I am tired of it!" She says, stalking off with her stack of tablets. You feel heat rising to your face.

As soon as Dresdale turns away Peter turns his gaze on you. The fake smile is gone. You look away and pretend that you are busy working on a locust net for Ediug.

"You better not have said anything!" Peter admonishes, quietly but with intensity as he too leaves the pod.

You sit and work on the net for a long time, and then you spend the day with Ediug, trying to put your little social problems behind you. That night, you come back to the pod to see that all of Dresdale's stuff has been moved out. You begin to fill with dread.

"She moved to her own pod," Peter tells you when you come in. Acid fills your stomach and the hunger that had been clawing at you moments ago disappears. "Thanks, thanks a lot! You're a real friend. Telling my secrets and stuff. Like it isn't bad enough that I don't have any parents, and now I find that I can't trust my best friend. Thanks!"

"But, I didn't, I mean, I never told her anything," you lie.

"Come on, you know you did. She told me you told her I liked her."

"Uh…"

"Yeah, 'uh,' how about, 'I'm sorry I'm such a jerk. Sorry that I broke your trust. Sorry I'm such a liar.' How 'bout that!"

"I am sorry," you say, but at that moment you know there's nothing you can say or do to make it up to him. Anger at Dresdale starts to burn in you. She promised!

You spend the next few days trying to apologize to Peter while giving Dresdale the cold shoulder, but mostly spending time with Ediug, working your body and learning the secrets of the wilds of the inner world. However, the tension between you and Peter rises to such a level that he moves to his own pod after two days of barely speaking to you. You feel so strange, in this bizarre world, surrounded by alien creatures, and now cut off from your friends, your only link to the relative normality of the surface world. The Illuminated don't know quite what to make of the new split among the humans, but they acquiesce to the demand for separate sleeping quarters.

Ediug, trying to be a friend, lets you sleep at his place, but it's not the same.

By the time the Desera come back, things have changed dramatically.

"War has spread fast, like a cancer across this land. Soon all routes into Agartha will be closed," Relevart announces when you meet him in the darkness of the womb-like cave. The Desera stand still and silent. They sniffed at you and yipped in a way that sounded approving when translated into a grunt by the crystal around your neck. "You will have to travel quickly if you hope to find your parents, Child of the Child."

Not surprisingly, neither Peter or Dresdale will come with you on your mission.

"I have to stay with Neila," Peter says without anger, and without the possibility of a mind change.

"This is a fool's errand," Dresdale tells you. "I've been talking to Relevart too, and there is no way that you can make it into Agartha now."

"I'm sorry that I took Peter's anger at me out on you," you say.

"Whatever. Don't treat your friends like dirt."

"I'm sorry. I hope you know that." You sigh. "Good luck with the translating."

Dresdale is correct. By the time that you make it to the border of Agartha, the war has spread and that there is no possibility of making it into enemy territory unnoticed. Also, the route back to The Illuminated's outpost is cut off by a surprise move by the Agarthans into their territory. Peter, Dresdale, Neila, and the rest are safe for the moment, but they are under siege, and you are caught in the middle of a Desera war camp. Helpless and useless to the people involved in the war, you spend your days working on fixing anything you can, carrying messages and doing other menial tasks.

Weeks fade into months, and there is no word about your parents. It seems like they have been swallowed up by this gigantic hole in the ground that turned into a complete world filled with both wonder and war.

The End

The Crystal Net

Y ou scramble to think of something, anything, to cover for your slip-up. You're not willing to break Peter's trust by telling Dresdale that he has a crush on her.

"I mean interest in your translation project," you mumble. "I think he wants to help, but thinks that you'll make fun of his efforts or something..." It sounds pretty lame to you, but you leave it at that.

"Really? You think that he just wants to help?" Dresdale's voice is earnest as she continues. "I would never make fun of him if he were trying to help. I'm not like that!"

"I know," you agree. "Boys are weird that way though. Anyway, how do you think we can get to the Lemurians at Lighthome if the Desera don't come?"

"I've been giving that some thought. Why can't we do something else? We don't even really know where your parents are. Maybe there is someone else besides the Lemurians who can help us."

"Like who?" you ask.

"Well, the book I have been translating talks about The Illuminated working with other groups. Most of it is still pretty rough, but they talk about another desert group called 'the People' or sometimes 'the Water Hunters.' It's all a bit vague, as The Illuminated talk about things in an abstract way. I really could use Peter's help with the project—I think it may help us find out more about what is going on here. I mean, before last week, I had no idea the Earth was actually hollow!"

"Me either," you agree. "Let's head back to the pod, I'm getting cold now that the sun has dimmed."

You walk back in silence, trying not to look directly at the dimmed sun above you. Even in its nighttime phase the light stabs at your eye like a shining pin if you look at it directly. Unlike the normal sun of the surface world, the inner sun is so small its presence is evident by a point so small it seems like what you imagine a singularity to be like. Ediug has told you that the sun's intensity has fluctuated erratically over the last ten years or so.

"The rumor is that Sceptus is controlling the sun," Ediug had told you as he gathered moss from a damp little grotto. "That's what is giving him the food, the water and the power to wage his wars of conquest. Who knows, though? I am not privy to the senior councils. But who wants to be inside a cave all day long? Not me!"

You glance at the burning red speck once more before going into your pod. It still feels a bit like a kid's playhouse to you, but you have to admit, it is more spacious and comfortable than your room at boarding school. The seniors always got the best rooms. You were hoping to get the one with the big old windows and the view of the mountains, but you doubt that will ever happen to you now. You don't even care, really.

The light of the pod is warm and comforting as you walk

in. You wonder if The Illuminated use lamps themselves or if they just use the light from their bodies.

"It's okay, Peter, I know why you've been acting so funny lately. We talked about why you were staring at me and making fun of me. And it's fine—cute even," Dresdale says blithely as she hangs her towel to dry. Peter gets up from his bed and shoots a death stare at you. You shake your head. Peter says nothing.

"It's nothing to be ashamed of," she continues. "I would never make fun of you for what you do or feel." You think she might be toying with you, but that is not like Dresdale, so you wait it out. "So, what I'm saying is, I would be happy to have your help with the translation project! Just so you know, I think you'll be a great help. I mean, you've spent so much time with Neila, you know tons of words that I don't."

"Yeah, uh, sure, that sounds great," Peter says, a bit confused.

"We should get some sleep now. I am beat from following Ediug all day. For a little guy, he can cover a lot of ground."

"I was going to stay up for a bit and work on the translation," Dresdale says. "Peter, I'd love some help if you feel like it. I know you were helping with Neila all day. How is he, anyway?"

"He's doing a lot better," Peter says, brightening and moving closer to Dresdale. She opens the book she has been translating and sets it on the low table. You head to the bathroom to warm up and get some clean clothes. Once you're out of earshot, you let out a huge sigh of relief.

When you come out, Peter and Dresdale are huddled over

an illustration in the book. They look up at you, smile, laugh, and go back to the book.

"G'night guys," you say to get their attention for a little bit. "Good night!"

"Yeah, catch you in the morning!"

Your legs ache from the hiking and swimming, but your mind won't let go. You lay on your back and think about your mom and dad, and tears roll out of your eyes. They form a trail down to your ears. You need to do something to get your parents back, but what? Peter says something indecipherable and Dresdale laughs quietly. Your tears stop and you feel something else. Something unpleasant. You turn over and lie as still as possible, willing yourself to fall asleep. As you do, your stomach growls and you realize you never ate dinner...

You dream that you are searching for your parents in a supermarket. You are also there to buy the ingredients for a dinner. You think the guests are supposed to be The Illuminated or the Radiant Ones, but you're not sure which. People keep telling you that you are in the wrong aisle when you ask for help, and by the time you check out, without your parents, the cashier tells you that your coupons are invalid and you have to put everything back. You find Peter and Dresdale in the cereal aisle, laughing about something, and not doing anything to help.

"Hey, wake up," Dresdale says gently, rubbing your shoulder. "You were shouting. Are you okay?"

"Mmph...fine. Just a nightmare. Well, not really fine, but

you know what I mean."

"We found out some cool things last night!" Peter says, coming around so you can see him. "Like how the communication net that Relevart uses to talk to the other Illuminated can transport people!"

"What are you talking about?"

"It's really cool, but we don't know for sure yet," Dresdale cautions. "We're going to talk to Neila and the others about it this morning. We'll let you know the scoop."

"That's great, guys. Thank you for all your help. I really mean it."

"We know. That's why we're here," Peter says, tapping Dresdale on the shoulder. "We should get going."

You scramble out of bed as soon as they leave. Ediug gave you a set of desert camouflage robes. You have to watch your hands carefully as you unfold the robes and slide them over your head. The material is so light and insubstantial that your fingers can barely feel it, but it is thick enough to block all of the light from Ediug's glowing body. There is even a veil. Yours has been altered to allow room for your bigger body.

"Since you do not glow; it will not be a problem," Ediug tells you when you meet him at the top of the trailhead to the desert floor.

You have a love/hate relationship with the trail. One part of you knows that the daily trips have been making your body strong, but you have a fear of the steep climb up at the end of a long day. Ediug just climbs it like it's a short flight of stairs.

"Today we hunt locusts," he tells you with a flourish, as he unfurls a net between two poles. He points to two tall baskets with straps. "We need to fill these up for the feast."

"What feast?" you ask, taking one of the poles and getting a feel for the net. "What is it for?"

"I don't know why, but they told me to fill these two baskets with locusts. I don't mind, I love locusts."

You can't see Ediug's face behind his robes, but you hear his lips smacking and the sound of his sharp teeth clacking together is like a woodpecker on a hollow tree. The thought of locusts for dinner doesn't exactly thrill you, but being so hungry you're up for just about anything. By and large, you have enjoyed the food the Illuminated have shared with you. You immediately fell in love with the mushroom steaks, and the various sweet mosses and root vegetables were tender and tasty, but a large portion of the Illuminated diet seemed to consist of all types of insects.

Peter had no problem with it, and in fact he would make a big show of grabbing something squirmy or crunchy and eat it right in Dresdale's face. One time she punched him, hard, and he didn't do that anymore.

You follow Ediug down the cliff, and onto the plateau. He takes you to an area you have never been before. It is a sort of scrubland instead of a true desert. You don't see any flowing water, but you do see dense thickets of brush and the occasional small tree. Ediug sets you up with one of the poles holding the net and takes the other and sets it securely in the loose earth at the mouth of a narrow gully. Even though you know it is there, you can barely see the net. Ediug creeps towards the other end of the gully, being careful not to disturb any animals or insects while doing so.

As people, and apparently, Illuminated, have done for thousands of years, you and Ediug take sticks, beat the bushes and make as much noise as possible to scare your prey into waiting death. By the time you get to the net, it is quivering and rasping from the activity of the trapped locusts. Ediug carefully removes a caught bird from the net, wraps the two poles together, and trots off with his buzzing haul over his shoulder.

"Wait up," you yell, laughing and trying to keep up.

Later on, you find out the reason for the feast.

"Come on, guys!" you whine at the door of your little pod. "We're gonna be late!"

"We are not, besides, I know the reason for the celebration," Peter says smugly, lightly arranging his hair with one of the Illuminated's tiny brushes.

"One, you are a liar, because earlier you said you didn't know. Two, you are getting addicted to our little friends' bathroom over there. You spend half your life in there. Even Dresdale mentioned it."

"Hey, sometimes perfection takes time," he says. "But I admit I was lying earlier when I said that I didn't know the reason. You know, it's a secret and everything."

"You suck," you reply, getting up and leaving. "I'm not waiting for you any longer."

"Well, perfect timing, 'cause I'm ready!"

The dinner, locusts included, is wonderful. You look up at the small table set in the middle of a bowl-shaped room where

Relevart, Peter, and Neila are sharing their meal and many jokes. Peter makes a trilling whistle that you would swear was made by one of the Illuminated; your crystal translates it as "the bristly end of a witch's broom." The three of them laugh; it makes no sense to you but it makes you smile to see them having fun. It reminds you of how badly in need you are of a healthy dose of lightness and humor. You can't remember the last time you laughed heartily.

"Thank you to our friends," Relevart says after the eating is done. He tosses a small pile of inedible insect shells and bits into the fire pit. He watches the flames for a moment before standing and putting his glowing hands together. "Without your help, we would have lost more than Legna and Setirps to the Radiant Ones."

A pulse of guilt flashes through you at the mention of the two Illuminated who died in Carlsbad Caverns. You had not thought of them for a while, caught up in your own thoughts and cares. Unlike Neila, you only knew them briefly before they were taken by the burning monsters coming after you all. Somehow Peter had been able to pick Neila up and get away. You left them behind and they died. Dresdale reaches over and gives your shoulder a squeeze. She was there—she knows.

"But tonight, we are here to celebrate! Neila has made a full recovery! Our guide is with his people! Without your help this would not have been possible. We would have been without our light-shiner, our glow of life in the darkest cave."

After that, The Illuminated sing songs, perform intricate light shows with their dancing bodies, and drink lots of boiling hot fermented tea. Everyone has a good time, including Neila, who never stops smiling. Luckily you were able to wrap your guilt and sadness into a tidy package and set it aside, so that, at least for Neila's sake, you could enjoy the festivities.

In the morning, instead of Ediug coming to meet you, it was an Illuminated whom you'd never seen before.

"Please come to the cave to see Relevart," she says. At least you think this one is female. You can never be sure with The Illuminated.

As always, entering the deep part of the cave is like draping light velvet curtains over your mind's eye. Your body moves normally, but it seems less physical, removed from reality.

"Thank you for coming so quickly," Relevart says. He is sitting in the middle of a half-circle of glowing Illuminated. Neila is on his left side, pulsing with a bluish light. "With the return of Neila to the circle, we can open the crystal gateway. These are focal points between two places."

"We see crystal point!" Neila adds in his piping English. "In caves."

"We have been in contact with the Lemurians. They have a small outpost in one of the deepest caves. It is a focal point, and we can use the crystal gateway to bring you there."

You have many questions, but you only ask one.

"Thank you! When can we leave?"

"Tomorrow. We need to arrange it with the Lemurians. Communication has been difficult recently, but seems to be better now. The outpost is a full day's travel away from

Lighthome, their capital, but the roads are all currently held by the Lemurians, so you should have no problems getting there. Hopefully they can help you find your parents!"

"Do you think Relevart could have transported us to the Lemurian outpost before Neila got better?" Dresdale asks you as you pack your few belongings into your backpack.

"Maybe," you reply. "Now that you mention it, I mean. There is something about him that makes me, I don't know, uneasy is too strong a word. Maybe it's that he puts his people first. I can understand that, though. Anyway, it doesn't really matter. If he can get me closer to finding my parents, then I plan on thanking him sincerely."

Ediug gives you a black crystal knife in a leather sheath. Although only about an inch and a half long, the blade is sharp. Ediug used it to skin small game, eat his food and scrape spines off cacti. If it didn't glow slightly, you would think it was obsidian.

"Thank you," you say. Taking his hand in yours, you hug him. You are surprised when tears come.

This time when you enter the cave, there is a full circle surrounding one of the larger crystals in the back of the room. The Illuminated sing and chirp in their high voices and their bodies glow and pulse in rhythm with the song. It is beautiful yet at the same time, rather unnerving.

"I'll be able to come back and see Neila, right?" Peter asks again. None of the Illuminated stops to answer him, so Dresdale steps in.

"That's what Relevart said, Peter. After transporting us through and making sure we are safe with the Lemurians, Neila will come home and rest some more while we move on to Lighthome, the Lemurian's capital. Don't worry, this should be fun! We're going to travel via a crystal network!"

"Well, excuse me for wanting to know a few more details before I get broken down into bits and then re-configured. If Neila wasn't taking us, I wouldn't be going!"

"Yeah, we know, you told us before," you say, although you too are scared about the being-transformed-into-energy part.

"Come on, Relevart is motioning us to come forward," Dresdale says brightly.

The pale blue light pulsing from the crystal bathes your hands in warmth. Your hands tingle as you reach forward and you stumble when your hands are not stopped by the surface of the crystal.

"You're falling into it!" Peter yells.

Neila pats you on the shoulder and reaches his hand into the crystal next to yours. Then, like a little kid struggling to get out of a swimming pool, he manages to swing his legs over the dull ledge of grey rock surrounding the crystal. He disappears completely inside the crystal. You soon feel a tug on your hand from within.

"This is so freaky!"

"Shh, Peter, they're trying to sing! Come on, you're next."

You follow Neila into the glowing crystal. Everything is blue inside. You are blue, Neila is blue and sparkly, and soon Peter and Dresdale are with you and blue as well. You can vaguely see Relevart and the other Illuminated through the flat surface of one of the crystal's panes.

Your mouth moves, but no sound comes out.

Neila takes your hand, you take Peter's, and you follow him deeper into the crystal. You walk as though through blue water. Ripples of light sparkle as you move. The sight is beautiful and a bit distracting—you imagine that if you let go of Neila's hand you could easily get lost. Everything looks the same to you—it is hard to distinguish things in the wash of blue—and sometimes it is hard to tell that you are even moving. Occasionally a flat pane like the one you just saw in the cave floats by as if pulled by some invisible line. Three of the panes have views of caves not that different from the one you left, but one shows the center of a city square, with people bustling about. You strain to catch a better view, but Neila pulls you forward and the view is lost.

Then Neila stops in front of one of the other floating panes. He reaches up and puts your hand on the rim and gives you an encouraging pat. You pull yourself through the window into the real world, and flop awkwardly to the floor, banging your elbow in the process. Then Peter lands on top of you.

"Ow!"

"Thanks for catching me," he says with a grin as he helps you up with one hand while using the other to make Dresdale's entrance more controlled.

You look around and are startled to see three huge men wearing black uniforms pointing guns at you.

"Hey, easy fellas," Peter says, noticing the guns. "I know that this is a military outpost, but you guys should be expecting us."

One of the men yells something at you and motions with his gun.

"Lie on the floor, now!" comes the translation from the crystal around your neck.

"Peter!" Neila yells, only his face is out of the crystal, the rest of his small body is still within. "Not Lemurians!! Agarthans!! Come with me!"

"What?"

Peter moves to take Neila's now outstretched hand, but before he can reach it, one of the Agrathan soldiers steps forward and knocks Peter to the floor with the butt of his rifle. Neila pops his head back into the crystal just as the soldier brings the rifle-butt down onto the crystal.

"No!"

Fragments of broken crystal cut your face as it explodes with a force and energy of its own. Without the crystal's glow, the room is darkened, and you stand there, stunned, until you get tackled by one of the soldiers and shoved to the ground. Even as he secures your hands behind your back, your mind becomes obsessed with questions old and new.

Did Relevart sell you out? How did the Agarthans get into the Lemurian crystal cave? Where are your parents?

Continued in *The Golden Path: Volume III, Paying the Ferryman*.

First Do No Harm

I'll go with you," Peter offers. "Dres and Rimy can care for Durno better than we can. They've been doing most of it already."

"I must go after them!" you explain.

"Good luck," Rimy responds. "We will do our best. I'm sure he will be fine."

"Glad I'm not the one hurt, maybe you'd leave me behind too," Dresdale says sourly, before adding. "Just kidding. Good luck."

"Yeah, catch you later."

You look behind you at Rimy, Durno, and Dresdale. You feel guilty about leaving them behind, but you have a burning desire, a need to find your family and make it whole once more.

"They'll be fine," Peter says, as you hike in a world that is alien and hostile.

You head into the wilderness of this strange inner world with only your friend Peter to help you through. It's a mistake. You are captured, half-starved and almost blind from the burning of the inner sun. Seeing that you are not Lemurians, you are conscripted into the Agarthan army. You and Peter spend most of your days digging trenches and earthen embankments. Red dust is your world. You wait for your chance to escape and begin your quest for your parents again. You wait a long time.

The End

Two Paths in a Wood

In for a penny, in for a pound,'" you say, letting go your hopes of finding your parents soon.

"Wrong expression, guv'nah, it should be 'all for one, and one for all!'" Dresdale corrects good-naturedly. "Besides, how long has it been since there was a pound?"

"You knew what he meant. Quit hassling!" Peter says, defending you.

"Who's zoomin' who?" Dresdale responds, and all three of you break out laughing. Rimy smiles.

The next day you trek backwards with the wounded Durno. Your journey is slow and difficult, but you make it to a village late in the day. They give you food, water, and shelter for the night, but they don't have a doctor or any medicine to help Durno.

You move on, figuring that your parents are probably going in the exact opposite direction of you. You realize that you have to abandon your plan to find them sooner rather than later. Letting go is hard for you, but you work on it. You are thankful for the company of your friends, and come to accept the need of the group for your strength and help.

"We'll find them eventually, I know we will," Dresdale says

to you at the end of the day.

"Maybe, I hope so, but I don't know anymore," you say, trying to face reality. "I don't know if we will find them. This place is so crazy I don't know...well, I do know that I couldn't have gotten this far without the help of all my friends. No way could I have left you guys behind. You're part of my family too."

Peter doesn't say anything. He lifts himself up from the ground with painful weariness and gives you a huge hug.

"You're my family," he says as he lets you go. "You're all I have. I would do anything for you guys."

"Me too," Dresdale agrees.

You may not ever find your parents, but you won't stop looking. You do have the gift of true friendship.

It is not the Golden Path, but it is a path of honor, and you have friends to accompany you. You are not alone.

The End

Big Sur

I don't think so," you say to the men in the black boat. Waves rock the vessel and water splashes onto the dock. You back up slowly and motion Dresdale and Peter to come with you. "I don't know who you are, or where you want to take us."

"Don't be a fool!" The man yells to be heard above the surf. "Do you have any idea of how many people put their lives on the line just so you could be met here?"

"No. No, I don't know, how could I?" you answer calmly as you move farther away. "I don't know them, and I don't know you, and I'm not getting in the boat. We'll take our chances on our own." Talking back to this stranger feels good, as if you are doing something right, something good, something for yourself, instead of giving in to adults who want to control you.

"Fools. Fools. Fools," the stranger says, shaking his head, "you'll be picked up by the Gatekeepers in no time. They're already on their way. This is your one chance to get away. I should just grab you and bring you with me."

"Listen, mister," Dresdale says in a strong, clear voice, "we're not going with you and if you try and force us, you'll be sorry. Come on, let's get out of here."

"Done and done," Peter says as he starts the flyer. "Hop in!"

You scramble into the back seat of the flyer, and Peter moves out of the way to let Dresdale take the controls. "Get us out of here, Dres, now!"

You are slammed back into the cushions by the force of the takeoff. When you look down, you see that the men in the black boat have gone inside their vessel. Zipping like a flying fish on top of the waves, it races out of view and you turn your attention back to the flight plan.

"Um, hate to bother you, but where are we going?" Dresdale says in a half-joking, half-scared tone. "I didn't like the looks of that dude, but I think he was right about the Gatekeepers."

"Since when do you say 'dude'?" Peter asks with mock amazement in his voice.

"Since I am really stressed out and trying to figure out what to do!! North, south, east or west?!"

"Sorry, Dres," you say, bringing yourself back to the task at hand. "Let's head inland and find a place to hide. Maybe in the mountains?"

"Okay, but let's do it quick. Oh no! What's that?" Dresdale shouts, pointing to two specks flying over the mountain ridge in front of you.

The black specks have lights that blink in pairs on their fronts like the two crows of omen—memory and sorrow. You feel your belly tighten in fear as they streak for you in the morning sun.

"Dres, take us down! Those are Gatekeeper interceptors!" Peter yells, but she is already diving for the perceived safety of the ground.

The landing is hard, so hard that you are stunned for a

moment, but you are not seriously injured. Peter pulls you from the back seat and you scramble to get away from the flyer and into the cover of the scrub trees.

"Keep moving!"

"I am!"

"Down this bank! It looks like there is a cave on the other side of the stream—we can hide in there."

The three of you huddle in the darkness of the wet cave. It is small and cramped and you each try to worm your way as far away from the opening like puppies searching for their mother, blind and needy. However, it is grown dogs that sniff you out.

With the first bay of a bloodhound, you know that you are caught, and it is just a waiting game until they come and get you from your hidey-hole. The men and women dressed in black are not gentle, but they are overly rough with you when they do pull you out. No one says anything. You are filled with regret for your bad decision.

"I'm sorry guys, I guess we should have gotten in the boat," you say as they load you into the back of one of the interceptors.

They question you for days, weeks, months, almost a full year. Eventually they let you go, finally convinced that you don't know much. But they watch you. Everywhere you go, they watch you, waiting for you to lead them to the ones they want.

The End

ABOUT THE ILLUSTRATOR

Vladimir Semionov was born in August 1964 in the Republic of Moldavia, of the former USSR. He is a graduate of the Fine Arts Collegium in Kishinev, Moldavia as well as the Fine Arts Academy of Romania, where he majored in graphics and painting. He has had exhibitions all over the world, in places like Japan and Switzerland, and is currently art director of the SEM&BL Animacompany animation studio in Bucharest.

CREDITS

Many thanks to R. A. Montgomery and Shannon Gilligan for major help with plot, storylines, and editing. Many thanks to Melissa Bounty for editing, managing and shepherding this book to completion. Her help has been invaluable. Thanks to Nina Jaffe for proofreading. Thanks also to Nancy Taplin for her beautiful paintings, and to Dot Greene and Stacey Boyd for book design.

ABOUT THE AUTHOR:
ANSON MONTGOMERY

After graduating from Williams College with a degree specialization in ancient history, Anson Montgomery spent ten years founding and working in technology-related companies, as well as working as a reporter for financial and local publications. In the past year he has returned to writing full-time. He is the author of four books in the original *Choose Your Own Adventure* series, *Everest Adventure, Snowboard Racer, Moon Quest* (reissued in 2008 by Chooseco), and *Cyber Hacker*. With *Choose Your Own Adventure® The Golden Path*™, he combines his interests and knowledge of ancient civilizations with his passion for science fiction, and fantasy. Anson lives and works in Warren, Vermont with his family.